ON ETRUSCAN TIME

To Joseph
Happy Birthday! 2006
Oma & Opa

TRACY BARRETT

ON ETRUSCAN TIME

Henry Holt and Company
New York

*Many thanks to Professor Barbara Tsakirgis of Vanderbilt
University for checking the terminology and techniques used
by my archaeologists, and the facts about the Etruscans.
Any errors that have crept in despite her care are my own.
And many thanks to my tireless and sensitive editor, Reka Simonsen.*

Alla memoria di Giancarlo e Benedetta Galassi Beria

Henry Holt and Company, LLC
Publishers since 1866
115 West 18th Street
New York, New York 10011
www.henryholt.com

Henry Holt is a registered trademark of Henry Holt and Company, LLC
Copyright © 2005 by Tracy Barrett
All rights reserved. Distributed in Canada by H. B. Fenn and Company Ltd.

Library of Congress Cataloging-in-Publication Data
Barrett, Tracy.
On Etruscan time / Tracy Barrett.—1st ed.
p.   cm.
Summary: While spending the summer on an archaeological dig near
Florence, Italy, with his mother, eleven-year-old Hector meets an Etruscan
boy who needs help to foil his treacherous cousin's plan to make him a
human sacrifice—2,500 years in the past.
ISBN-13: 978-0-8050-7569-4
ISBN-10: 0-8050-7569-0
[1. Archaeology—Fiction.   2. Etruscans—Fiction.   3. Time travel—
Fiction.   4. Mothers and sons—Fiction.   5. Human sacrifice—Fiction.
6. Italy—Fiction.]   I. Title.
PZ7.B275355On 2005
[Fic]—dc22   2004052341

First Edition—2005 / Book designed by Amy Manzo Toth
Printed in the United States of America on acid-free paper. ∞
1 3 5 7 9 10 8 6 4 2

"The distinction between past, present, and future is only an illusion, however persistent."

—Albert Einstein

1

Hector woke with a start. Had he cried out? He glanced at his mother, but her face mask was in place over her eyes, and her seat was still pushed back as far as it would go. So he couldn't have made any noise.

He settled back on the hard blue cushion, his heart pounding, and tried to steady his breathing. The nightmare was already fading, and he made no effort to remember it. Whatever it was had left him soaking in cold sweat, and he'd just as soon let it slip away to wherever dreams go.

He pressed his face against the tiny window, but all he could see was the reflection of his own dark eyes. His father had once told him that the best place to see stars was either in the middle of the desert or over the ocean, where the light from cities wouldn't drown them out. But even though someone had dimmed the cabin after the movie, he still couldn't see anything out there. The vibration of the jet traveled from the window down his face, tickling his nose, so he gave up, leaned back in his seat, and pushed his bangs off his forehead.

The plane ride was boring and long and uncomfortable, but it was just the beginning of what was going to be a terrible summer. Hector had argued and argued that he didn't want to go away. After a year in Tennessee, he wasn't the new kid anymore. He wanted to hang out with the boys who were finally his friends, swimming and skateboarding and playing computer games. He swore that he wouldn't get in his father's way while he worked. But they hadn't listened to him. No one ever listened to him. It was as if they couldn't even hear him.

The real reason he was going, he thought bitterly, was that they didn't know what else to do with him. Everyone else's plans had been more important than his, as usual, so he was just shoved aside to where he wouldn't be a nuisance. His father was working on a screenplay that his agent had said sounded promising, and his sister, Ariadne, was spending most of the summer with her friend Sarah in Florida, where they were working together in Sarah's mother's stationery store. And when his mother's friends had asked her to come stay with them and help out with a problem they were having, of course she said yes, even though that meant that Hector would have to go too. Whether he wanted to or not.

So he sat in the prickly airplane seat without even any stars to watch and looked out the window, waiting for the dawn to come. The sky turned pink, then green, then brilliant blue. The cabin lights came back on, and someone put a tray with a roll and cheese on it in front of him. After what seemed like hours, the landing gear dropped with a shudder that made him jump, and then they were rushing down a long runway.

His mother sat up and ran her hands through her hair. She turned to him and smiled. "Welcome to Italy, Heck," she said.

Hector slumped in a hard plastic chair while they waited for their bags. His head felt so hot and thick that he was afraid of falling asleep and sliding to the floor if he closed his eyes, so he forced himself to look around. All the signs were in Italian, even the ones with familiar American logos on them. Hertz Autonoleggio. Holiday Inn Alloggio.

Their suitcases finally thumped down the slide onto the conveyor belt, and they wrestled them onto a cart. His mother pushed it, with Hector trailing behind, into a room marked "Dogana-Douane-Customs," where two bored-looking men waved them through into another, larger room that was crowded with people.

Someone called out, "Betsy!" and a tall blond woman flung her arms around his mother. His mother squealed back, "Susanna!" and kissed her on both cheeks, and then they hugged and laughed and talked in a mixture of Italian and English. His mother was explaining why the plane was late, and the other woman was saying that it was okay. They seemed to have forgotten that he was there.

He stood back, feeling fuzzy-headed and out of place in the crowd of Italians. His mother finally remembered him. "This is Hector, Susi," she said, and the woman reached down—despite her height she was wearing high heels—and gave his hand a brisk squeeze. "So pleased to meet you, 'Ector," she said. "You look just like your pictures."

He nodded, wondering if he was supposed to say something, but the tall woman turned back to his mother and started talking about the archaeological dig and the town they were going to. Half her words were in Italian, and the half that were in English were pronounced so strangely that he gave up trying to understand what she was saying and leaned against a post as Susanna went to get her car.

They tossed their bags into the tiny trunk, and his mother held the front seat forward so he could squeeze into the back. His legs jumped as they touched the hot upholstery. He slid over to the section that had been in the shade.

They stopped once at a kind of truck stop along the highway, and Hector's mother bought him a sandwich and a soda. He went to the bathroom while they were paying for gas, and it took him a long time to figure out that he had to push a button on the wall to make the toilet flush.

The food looked terrible. But when he settled back into his seat and Susanna took off at what felt like a million miles an hour, his first reluctant nibble of the sandwich and swig of the soda took him by surprise. They were so full of flavor that he ate and drank slowly, prolonging the pleasure as the thin ham melted on his tongue and the sweetness of the soda intensified the meat's saltiness.

It was hot in the car, despite the open windows, and Hector fought to keep his eyes open. He lay on his back as well as he could with the seat belt pinching his middle, his feet up on one armrest and his head, cushioned by his arm, on the other. He stared out the window from between his knees.

He didn't realize he'd fallen asleep until a jolt woke him. He sat up, his eyes gritty and his mouth dry, and looked outside. While he was sleeping, dark clouds had rolled in, and it looked as if it were about to rain. They had left the highway and were winding up the side of a hill on a narrow road. His mother and Susanna were quiet.

"Where are we?" he asked.

"Oh, you are awake," Susanna said. "This is Sporfieri, the little city where the archaeologists live while we are working. Our house is—" and she gestured up the hill.

Another jolt. The road switched back and forth up the slope. A wall of huge dark stones seemed to hold up the hillside rising next to them. By twisting his neck and peering upward, he could see houses clustered above. The small buildings squatted comfortably next to each other. Yellow light came from some of the windows, and there was the occasional flicker of a TV set.

They pulled up in front of a narrow house that looked just like all the others around it. How could Susanna tell one from the other? Hector and his mother yanked out their suitcases while Susanna fumbled with her keys.

But before she could open the door, it was flung open from inside by a tall, slender man with sandy hair and an ugly but smiling face. Hector's mom said, "Ettore!" and kissed both his cheeks.

"How are you, Betsy?" the man asked. He had less of an accent than Susanna did.

"Oh, you know," his mother said, and laughed. "We had to change planes twice, and we missed our connection in—"

Was she just going to talk to this guy and forget he even existed? But the man caught Hector's eye and took a step toward him, right hand outstretched.

"Hector!" he said, and shook hands vigorously. Hector looked questioningly at his mother. "We have the same name, you know," the man went on. "I'm Ettore," accenting the word on the first syllable, "Ettore Bartolozzi. I am an old friend of your mother's. I work with Susanna at the dig."

"Why are you here, Ettore?" Susanna asked.

"I came to tell you something, both of you. All of you," he corrected himself, smiling at Hector.

"Well?" Susanna said.

"We learned something while you were in Rome, Susi," Ettore said. "Something so strange that we can't really believe it. I knew you would be furious at me if I didn't tell you right away—"

"Ettore, speak," Susanna said. "What did you find?"

"You know that hole that we thought was for garbage?" Susanna nodded. "We analyzed some of the things we found in it. And it isn't garbage. Or at least not normal garbage." He paused, obviously enjoying the suspense he was creating.

"You want to guess what we found?"

"Ettore!" both women said at once.

"All right, all right," he said. "We found bones."

"So?" Susanna said. "Often there is bones in the garbage. Bones of pigs. Bones of sheeps. Bones—"

"Human bones," said Ettore.

2

Sometime in the middle of the night, Hector woke up and for an instant didn't know where he was. His eyes refused to focus. The room was dark, but there was enough light for him to see the door, the windows, the furniture. They were all in the wrong places. Then he remembered—he was in Sporfieri, in the little room next to his mother's. Everything whirled around in his head before settling down. There was the window facing the narrow street. Opposite it was the door leading to the hallway, and between them was the big piece of furniture that took the place of a closet.

He lay back down and sighed, feeling wide awake. Susanna had said he'd slept a long time in the car, and then after they had eaten the bread and fruit that Ettore had put out for them, he couldn't stay awake. He looked at the clock that glowed on his bedside table and did some quick math. Only eight o'clock at night at home, and he'd been asleep for hours. Weird.

Now what? The house was so small that if he turned on the TV in the tiny living room it would wake up his mother and Susanna, and anyway, he didn't think watching TV in Italian would be very interesting. He glanced at the book on his bedside table. No, he had the whole summer to read that.

He got up, though the stone floor was so cold that his toes curled in protest. He pushed open the heavy wooden shutters and looked out. The house they were sharing with Susanna was near the top of the hill, and below him he saw a few dozen small buildings, crammed together on the crooked streets. They reminded him of mushrooms—not in the way they looked, because they were square, not round—but because of the way they were clustered, like clumps of mushrooms on their lawn in Tennessee after a rain. And they looked as if they had grown there, instead of being built.

It was not quite silent. He heard a buzzing, like one of those motor scooters that had darted around their car, and the small sound of a radio or a TV came from someplace nearby. He heard men talking, sounding like they were giving orders, and a thud, like metal hitting wood. But that was all.

The moonlight turned the houses bluish silver instead of the yellow or brown they must be. Something about the light made them look fake, as if they were flat house fronts on a stage. He shivered a little and imagined something coming from behind them, some strange, dark thing. He leaned out the window and looked around. Nothing was out there, as far as he could tell. But you could never be sure. Those deep shadows could hide anything.

"Can't sleep?" Hector turned around quickly. But it was just his mother, wrapped in her bathrobe, her curly dark hair messy around her face. He suddenly wished he was little again so he could go bury his face in her soft robe. She would take him to bed and rub his back until he fell asleep. But he was eleven, and she hadn't done that for years.

He shook his head. "Me either," she said.

"What did that guy Ettore mean about human bones?" he asked.

"I don't know," she said. "They look human, but there isn't a specialist on the team here, so they sent the bones to a lab to be analyzed. We should find out more tomorrow. I mean today." She yawned. "I didn't stay up much later than you did, although I tried. But then when I went to bed I couldn't fall asleep. I drank so much coffee to stay awake and was so excited to see Susanna and Ettore that now I can't unwind. Anyway, it'll take a few days to get on Italian time."

"I wish we could just stay on Tennessee time," Hector said, knowing he was being unreasonable but wanting to keep her there talking a little longer.

"Time doesn't work like that," she said. "Once we start eating meals when everyone else does and going to bed when they do, we'll feel more comfortable, just as though we had always been on Italian time. And then when we go home, we'll have to adjust all over again."

He groaned, and she laughed. "I know," she said, reaching out and smoothing his hair. "But the sooner we get started, the easier it will be. Go back to bed and lie there with your eyes closed, at least. The sun will be up in a few hours, and that can be your signal that it's okay to get up. Will you try?" He nodded, and she said, "Goodnight, then," and went back to her room.

He lay still, but his eyes kept popping open. He forced them shut and said to himself, *I can open my eyes after I take a hundred breaths, but no fair cheating and breathing fast.* He started counting: *One, innnnnn . . . ooouuuuut . . . two, innnnnn . . . ooouuuuut . . .* In between counts, he pictured time zones spread around the world. He imagined the earth turning and the sun shining on some parts of the globe while others were in darkness. *Sixteen, innnnnn . . . ooouuuuut . . .* So if you traveled backward fast enough, would you wind up arriving earlier than when you left? Something was wrong with that, he knew, but as the globe twirled in his mind, he couldn't think what. *Twenty-eight, twenty-nine . . .*

When Hector woke again, a faint pinkish light was coming through the window. That meant the sun was rising and he could get up. He pulled on the clothes that were lying on the floor. He should probably unpack his suitcase, but there was plenty of time for that.

On his way down the hall, he paused and looked into his mother's room. She was still asleep, or at least still in bed. He thudded down the stone stairs. Susanna sat in the kitchen, wearing a bathrobe, her blond hair swept up loosely. She was reading a newspaper and sipping out of the tiniest cup he'd ever seen. *She must not like coffee very much*, Hector thought. But then why was she drinking it?

"Good morning, 'Ector," she said, laying down the paper. She looked as though speaking cost her an effort. His father was the same way in the morning.

"*Buongiorno*," he answered carefully, and was rewarded with a grin.

"Breakfast," she said, gesturing at the counter. "I don't know what you eat, so I bought some American food and some Italian food." There was a tiny box of cornflakes and a plate of brown rolls. They looked dry, but to be polite he picked one up. It was warm.

"They are new," Susanna said.

"Fresh?" Hector asked.

"Yes, fresh," Susanna said. "They make them there." She waved her hand vaguely in the direction of the street.

"They bake at night?" Hector asked.

"They make them all the night so we can have fresh bread," she said. "All but Sunday. Sunday morning we don't eat fresh bread, so the baker can sleep and go to church with his family."

That explained the voices and the clanking he had heard in the night. He took a bite of the roll. It was hollow, with a crust so crunchy that little bits flew all over the table. The inside of the crust was soft and delicious. He took another bite even before he'd swallowed the first one.

"That form of bread is called a *rosetta*," Susanna said. "It is the typical bread of Roma. Thousands of years ago the Etruscans made bread in that form. But you don't know about the Etruscans, I think."

"I do know a little," Hector said. "My mom gave me a book. They were people who lived in Italy more than two thousand years ago, before the Romans, right? And they had a mysterious language. My mom says that lots of the things that most people think the Romans invented, the Romans really learned from the Etruscans, like gladiators and aqueducts and telling the future by looking at the insides of animals."

"Very good," she said, nodding. "And the village of Sporfieri is built on top of a very, very antique Etruscan city. We archaeologists are here to learn about the people who lived in that city. Nobody knows very much about the Etruscans, so any small thing we find is a treasure. We don't—didn't—haven't found many good things. This is our last summer. The money for digging is almost gone."

"Is that why you asked my mother to come?"

"*Si*," she said. "When I and Ettore and your mother studied at the university in Roma together, your mother learned antique languages like *that*." Her quick finger-snap made Hector jump. "She has a facility for languages. We have found some things with letters on them, and we hope to find more. With your mother here—"

"With me here, what?" She came into the kitchen, still in her bathrobe. She poured herself a tiny cup of coffee and sat next to Hector. She spread a roll thickly with strawberry jam and took a bite.

"Ah, Betsy," Susanna said. "Did you sleep well?"

"No," she said around her bread. "It will take a few days. Right, Heck?" He nodded.

"We were talking about your facility for antique languages."

"*Ancient* languages," she corrected. "Hector inherited it, I think, at least for Italian. On the plane he could repeat back to me all sorts of things in Italian, when I just said them to him once."

"*Bravo*, 'Ector," Susanna said. "I wish I had a facility. And I hope you still have yours, Betsy."

"I don't know." His mother put down her coffee cup. "After years of teaching nothing but beginning Latin and Greek, I haven't been able to test it for a long time."

"Well, *we'll* test you," Susanna said, and she winked at Hector. "What is the original of the name of this town?"

"Sporfieri?" Hector's mother frowned in thought. "Let's see—*spor*; that part's easy."

"Why is that easy?" Hector asked.

"*Spur* is Etruscan for *city*," she explained. "We don't know a whole lot of words, but that one's certain. Now about the *fieri* part." She frowned in concentration, her head tilted to one side as though listening. She murmured, "*Fieri*—could that be *fler*?" she asked, looking at Susanna, who shrugged. "Why would they name this place that?"

"Name it what?" Hector asked.

"To turn into *fieri* in Italian," his mother went on, "the original Etruscan word must have been something like *fleris*. Maybe it was *flere*, which meant *god*. That could mean this was a holy city. But I don't think so. If it were some kind of sacred place, we probably would have heard about it before, and the Etruscan town under Sporfieri isn't mentioned by any writers. It's like it never existed."

"But—" Hector started. His mother went on as though she hadn't heard him. As usual.

"Or the Etruscan word could be *fler*, 'sacrifice.' But why would they name their whole town after sacrifice? They were doing them all the time, in every city, not just this one. So why name this particular town City of Sacrifice?"

"Maybe something was not usual about the sacrifices they made here," Susanna said.

"What about those bones?" Hector asked. Finally they looked at him, as though surprised he could talk. "Maybe they sacrificed people," he said.

3

The two women looked at each other. "Well," his mother said thoughtfully, "that would explain why no one mentions the town. If it was associated with something so terrible, maybe they were trying to forget it. And Susi, you know, some people say the Etruscans did perform human sacrifice. Remember that temple near Cortona, that one with the sphinxes devouring people? An article I read said that the statues could represent human sacrifice."

"I don't know," Susanna said doubtfully. "Professor Carberry says it, but nobody else."

"True," Hector's mother said, "but if a scholar of his standing—"

The door opened and Ettore's head poked around. *"Permesso?"*

"Caffè?" Susanna asked, waving at the coffee pot.

"Sì, grazie," he said, and poured himself a cup. Weren't they going to talk about the bones anymore? It was always the same. Just when things got interesting, the subject changed.

After breakfast, the adults took off at a brisk walk, talking quickly in Italian, and Hector followed slowly on the bumpy street made of flat, dark stones.

Now that the sun was up, the sky was bright blue and he could see that the houses were different shades of tan. They weren't very tall, and their shutters were closed against the sun, which was already warm after the night's chill. In the doorways, heavyset women in dark, tight dresses sat on folding chairs, talking to each other as they knitted or cut up vegetables. They didn't look too friendly, but when Hector passed by, they said, "*Ciao*" or "*Buongiorno*." When he answered in careful Italian they broke into smiles that made them look nicer. One or two even patted his shoulder and said, "*Bravo!*" at his Italian.

The road of smooth, flat stones went down and down. In a few places the adults in front of him took a shortcut on worn, gray steps that cut straight through the curves, instead of going back and forth like the road did. Hector followed at an ever-increasing distance. The steps were uneven and steep, and there was nothing to hold on to. He saw his mother run her hand down the house wall next to her to keep her balance, so he did the same. The stone was cold and felt wet under his touch, although his hand was dry when he took it off.

The third set of stairs ended in an arched opening in the dark stone wall that encircled the base of the hill, enclosing the town. The adults had already gone through it, and he quickened his pace so he could catch up, then stumbled on the black paving stones. He didn't fall, but he stopped for a second to regain his balance, then went on more carefully, watching his step. He emerged from the semidarkness into the brightness of the early-summer morning.

After blinking a few times as his eyes adjusted to the light, Hector saw that he was in a shallow valley. Rows of neon-orange sticks poked out of the ground, with strings attaching them to each other. Near one of these strings, Hector's mother stood with her hands on her hips, looking down into a hole in the ground and nodding while Ettore pointed into it and said something. Susanna interrupted, asking a question in a high, excited voice.

Hector turned and looked back toward the village squatting solidly on its hill. Another group of adults was coming out of the arched opening in the wall and heading toward them. The morning light slanting down the valley made their shadows look like small-headed giants moving bumpily across the field. He suddenly felt shy and didn't want to have to talk to them, even if they spoke English, so he trotted down to where his mother was now lowering herself into a rectangular trench.

"These are the same as the ones you've had analyzed?" she asked. Ettore nodded.

"*Si, si,*" he said. "We got the results by fax. Preliminary, but they seem sure."

"So they're definitely human?"

A grunt of assent.

The other people—the archaeologists, he supposed—had reached the dig area. There were six or eight of them, and most looked younger than Ettore and Susanna. They were dressed for the heat and the women's hair was tied back. Some were speaking English, some what sounded like German, and some Italian. He could pick out the Italian, even from this distance—the sounds were much rounder than in the other languages. They clustered, talking and laughing, at the door of a metal shed a short distance away. They went into the shed one at a time, emerging with small boxes.

Hector stood aside as Ettore introduced the people to his mother. She shook hands with each of them and then said something that made them laugh. They split up into different groups and started working. Some dug in the trenches, while others measured a piece of ground and marked off a square with string. They settled down, only occasionally calling out to each other. Someone turned on a radio that blared American music.

His mother was obviously too involved in what she was doing to pay any attention to him. So what was he supposed to do all day? All summer? He turned and looked down the path they had taken from the town—it went along the side of the dig and then disappeared around a little hill.

Odd-shaped trees stood all around. One kind had a

tall, branchless trunk that suddenly burst into a flat green canopy at the top, and another was long and skinny, its branches so tight that you couldn't see individual limbs. *Just like umbrellas*, he thought, *some open and some shut*.

Away on his left was a stand of silvery green trees. They were small, with leaves so close together that they created a dense shadow on the ground.

"Those are olive trees," said Ettore, who had appeared at his elbow.

"Olives grow on trees?" Hector asked.

"Certainly," Ettore said. "Where did you think they grew?"

Hector shrugged. He had never really thought about it. They tasted as if they were made in a factory.

"And there"—Ettore pointed past the olive trees—"are some grapevines, for the wine."

Hector didn't know what to say next. He glanced over at Ettore, who was looking at him thoughtfully.

"So, what are you going to do?"

"About what?" Hector asked.

"About today," Ettore answered. "Are you going to watch?" Hector shrugged. "Maybe," Ettore said, "maybe I could have you do some work. Would you like that?"

"What kind of work?"

"You could be an archaeologist," Ettore answered. "You could be a—what do you call an *apprendista*, some-one who works and learns at the same time?"

"An intern?"

"Something like that," Ettore said. "But more young, usually."

"Apprentice?"

"*Ecco,*" Ettore answered. "Would you like to be an apprentice archaeologist?"

"Sure," Hector said. "That would be great."

"Okay," Ettore said. "First I have to ask Susi. But I'm sure she'll agree." And he walked over to where Susanna was talking with Hector's mother.

Hector felt a surge of excitement. It had never occurred to him that he would actually get to do some archaeology. Suddenly the summer didn't look so bleak. What if he found a statue? A gold necklace? A house with paintings on the walls, like in Pompeii?

Ettore came back. "It's okay," he said. "Usually our apprentices are college students, but your mother says you're good at following directions, when you want to. True?"

"I guess so," Hector said. "What do I do first?"

Ettore showed him the toolshed and found him some spare instruments. He told Hector how important it was to stop and get Ettore or Susanna to look at anything he found before he moved it, and how fragile a lot of the old things were.

"First, look for a while," he said. "Then, maybe this afternoon, you can start work." So as Ettore responded to someone who called his name, Hector wandered around the dig, looking in one trench after another.

It was fascinating, what they were doing. One man was shaking dirt in a sieve. Another used a cloth to wipe a piece of what looked like a broken plate and then showed it to the woman next to him, who exclaimed at it before carefully sliding it into a plastic bag. Most of the people were sitting in trenches, scraping or brushing at the walls or floor. Ettore was pointing at something and talking to a freckled woman who was holding something that looked like a dentist's tool. She nodded as she scraped at the wall of the trench, saying, "*Sì, sì, d'accordo.*"

Ettore glanced up and saw Hector. He smiled, his homely face crinkling as he squinted into the sun.

"What do you think?" he asked.

"It looks so neat," Hector said. "What are they finding in there?" *The tomb of a powerful king? A treasure trove?*

"We're mostly getting broken pots in this place." *Oh. Broken pots.*

"We think it must have been like a garbage place," Ettore went on. "You see how it's far away from where people lived, so they didn't have to smell it from their houses."

Hector leaned over the edge, trying to see what was in there, and nearly lost his balance. Ettore grabbed his arm.

"*Attento!*" he said. "You'll fall and break some bones. Yours will heal, but the ones we have found don't know how to do that anymore." Hector backed up. All he could see in the trench were some knobby gray things. How could anyone tell what was something old and what was just ordinary stuff that you find in the ground?

This trench was only one of many, each with ruler-straight edges, marked off by the strings he'd seen earlier. On the orange stakes, numbers were written in black marker.

"We'll leave this place to Susanna," Ettore said. "She won't let anyone else touch the bones until she's finished with them."

"What's she going to do with them?" Hector asked.

"Remove them carefully, making notes and taking pictures to show in what position they are," he answered, leading Hector away from the trenches, down the path. "That way maybe someone can tell how the owner of the bones died and why his body was thrown in the garbage instead of being buried. The Etruscans, like all ancient peoples, were very careful to bury their dead in the correct way. It's one of the things that societies care about the most. So it's strange for a person to be treated like garbage, or like an animal."

Worse than an animal, Hector thought, remembering how carefully his father had buried their old dog, Zephyr, in their backyard last winter. The people in this village must have really hated the person whose bones Ettore had found.

Ettore stopped in the shade of a small tree. They were in a flat place not far from the trenches, where no one had dug anything.

"Susanna says you should start here," Ettore said. "We don't usually find things in places like this, and we don't think that the village came out in this direction. So you don't have to worry that you will accidentally ruin something. I can show you how to dig with care, and when you have proven to me that you know how to do it, Susi will let you in the trench." He handed Hector a small, pointed trowel, a fat paintbrush, a flat-bottomed sieve, and a notebook and stubby pencil.

"Now watch," he instructed, and with the point of his trowel began scraping at the red dirt. When he hit something hard, he worked around it, brushing away the loosened soil, until a rock slowly showed its shape.

"Just a stone," he said, pulling it out and tossing it aside. "But if it were something that looked interesting, you would stop and call me. You would make a note about where you found it and then sketch it."

"I'm not too good at drawing," Hector said.

"That's okay," Ettore assured him. "We have an artist who will make a good picture. And a photographer. You just need to show enough of what it looks like so that we can identify it later."

"How do I know if it's something interesting?"

"Well, if it looks as if a person made it. Like if there's a straight line. Or—" He sketched a shape in the air with his hands.

"A right angle? Like the corner of a square?"

"Exactly. You hardly ever find right angles and straight lines in nature. Or circles. So tell me if you find something round, except a golf ball or something like that. Also if you find something of a color that isn't the same as the dirt."

"Or if it's made of gold."

Ettore laughed. "Right, if it's gold then certainly stop and call me. And I will call Susanna, and she will call the newspapers. Now you take a turn."

Hector picked up the tools. The dirt was harder than he had thought and at first he scraped either too hard or not hard enough, but soon he was getting approving nods from Ettore. Small puffs of dust flew into the air, leaving grit in his teeth.

"The dirt down in the trench is a little different from this," Ettore said, "but you're learning the technique. Just practice for a while. And remember, call me if you find something interesting." He went back to his own work.

So Hector scraped and brushed, uncovering a few more rocks and a tree root. It wasn't very hard work, but it was hot in the sun, and it was getting kind of boring. A rivulet of sweat ran into his eye, stinging. All this work for a piece of a pot? What a long summer this was going to be. For a moment his mind wandered to the green hills of home, where his friends were probably staying up all night watching videos and spending all day at the lake.

Then, in the little hole he had dug, he felt a scrape against the tip of his trowel. He dropped it and picked up the brush. He swept dirt away from whatever it was, and something flashed at him so brightly that he had to squint to keep tears from coming to his eyes. What could be shining like that, under the dirt?

He put up his hand to shield his face from the blinding light. He felt a small twitch of fear deep in his belly, but stronger than the fear, stronger than the pain to his eyes, was an overwhelming desire to hold the thing that glowed. He felt like he was dying of thirst and the light was a glass of cold water. Like he was six years old and the shining thing was the best Christmas present in the world. He wanted it desperately, without knowing why or even what it was.

Carefully, he used the trowel to loosen the last bit of earth. He dropped the trowel and picked up the brush, smoothing away the powdery red dirt.

And the thing was revealed.

4

Hector reached toward the light, which was making his closed eyelids glow deep red, and his fingers curved around something smooth and cold and round.

As he gripped it, he was struck by how quiet everything was. Evidently somebody had turned off the radio, and the archaeologists must be too busy to talk. Still, out in the country like this, it was odd not to hear birds singing. And the leaves weren't rustling, even though a light breeze brushed against his skin. The only sound— and it was one he had not heard before—was the faint strumming of some stringed instrument, like a guitar, only muted. It seemed to come from all around him, and the notes excited him, although he couldn't have said why.

When he cautiously opened his eyes again, the bright light from the stone had gone out. It must have dazzled his eyes, though, because the colors around him were muted, gray and white. The olive trees seemed almost transparent—he could practically see the hills through them.

He turned to look back at the dig and rubbed his eyes. The toolshed looked like a shadow, and he would swear that he saw the faint outline of another, larger building near it. And who were those people walking around? They didn't look like the archaeologists. Were there really people there, or was it some trick of the light? He couldn't tell for sure.

He stood up, feeling like he was moving in slow motion. What was this? Was he having some new problem with the time change that made him groggy and slow? But he wasn't sleepy; he felt more wide awake and alert than he'd ever been before. It was just that the world around him looked faded. His fingers loosened, and the rock dropped out of his hand.

From down at the dig came a sudden burst of laughter, followed by quick chatter in a foreign language. The sound of the radio, playing an American rap song, was clear and loud. A motor scooter sped down the path from the town and buzzed out of sight around the hill. And now the day was bright again, with a warm yellow light that made everything look solid and comfortable. The toolshed stood squat and real, and there was no other building near it, not even an outline. The shadowy people were gone—of course, he told himself, they had never been there to begin with—and the only person walking around was Susanna, bending over trenches and talking to the people digging in them.

The exhilaration disappeared, and suddenly Hector felt as exhausted as at the end of field day at school. *What just happened here?* he thought, then shook his head to try to straighten out his mind. *Did I go to sleep and have a strange dream about a glowing rock?* But no, the stone lay on the ground in front of him. It was no longer dazzling—if it ever had been—and he picked it up and looked at it. It was just a chunk of white rock. Nothing out of the ordinary. But there was a hole near the tree root about the same size and shape as the rock, so he hadn't dreamed digging it up.

He rolled the rock around in his palm and saw that on the other side was a blue circle of stone surrounding a smaller black one. It looked like an eye. *Weird*, he thought. He glanced toward the dig and started to call Ettore but then reconsidered. *How can I tell him about the light?* he wondered. *And about the way that it felt like I just had to pick up that stone? He told me to call him as soon as I found anything interesting, and this sure is interesting. He might get angry that I didn't say anything.*

The exhaustion moved over him again, dragging his eyelids down, pulling his chin toward his chest. He sat down, leaning against the tree, the rock loose in his palm. *I'll just shut my eyes for a few minutes*, he thought. *And then I'll think of what to do.* Once again the world grew dim and sound faded away, but this time it was the familiar hazy sensation of normal sleep that was overtaking him.

He was standing at the edge of a crowd of people, gathered together in a tight but silent group. The light was clear but strangely pale, like when you open your eyes under water in a swimming pool.

Everyone was looking in the same direction, toward a brightly colored building that looked vaguely familiar to Hector as he turned to see what they were all staring at. It was larger than the other structures around it. Nobody was talking. Even the babies and small children were still.

Why were they all focused so intently? Hector screwed up his eyes and followed their gaze. The building looked kind of like the temples pictured in books on ancient Greece and Rome. A short flight of steps led up to a row of columns, which supported a peaked roof. A carved face with its tongue sticking out gazed with crossed eyes over the crowd from the point of the roof, and animals that looked like a mix between eagles and cats perched on the corners. Hector could just barely make out a closed door behind the row of columns, but it was in such deep shadow under the overhang that he couldn't see any of its details.

Unlike pictures of the old temples, all the different parts of this building were painted. The columns were blue and red, the details of the animals and the carved face were picked out in many colors, their edges outlined in black. It was so colorful that it almost hurt Hector's eyes in the unnatural light.

People were beginning to mutter and shift their weight from foot to foot, as though they were becoming impatient. A baby started to cry and was hushed.

Still, they all stared at the colorful building. The tension grew until Hector would have sworn he saw electric sparks shooting around the crowd.

And then the temple door burst open.

Hector sat bolt upright, his throat closed tight in panic. Had he screamed? He settled back against the bumpy tree, his heart pounding, and tried to steady his breath. Despite the bright sun, he felt a chill that started deep in his bones. He wished he'd stayed asleep just a little longer. He hadn't seen what was coming through the door, but whatever it was, it would have been better to see it than to wake up not knowing.

The strange eye-shaped rock was still in his hand. He stared at it and shuddered.

"Did you find something?"

It was Ettore. Mutely, Hector held out the eye. As Ettore took it from him, Hector warmed, as though a hidden sun had come out again. And he felt something else too. He had that odd sensation of having lived through all this before. What did his dad call it? Déjà vu.

"Greek," Ettore said. "Modern."

"How do you know it's not ancient?"

Ettore rolled the eye over in his hand. "It wasn't deep enough in the dirt," he said. "The Etruscan things are farther down. And anyway, the city seems to stop back there," and he pointed toward the trenches. Hector barely listened. The feeling of déjà vu was slipping away, and the more he tried to hold on to it, the faster it fled. He shook his head and blinked.

Ettore had evidently finished talking while Hector was feeling time slide around, because the man handed the stone back to him and squatted by the place where Hector had been digging. Hector held the odd thing, considering whether to throw it far away, but for some reason he couldn't bring himself to do it. Instead he slid it into his pocket and stood up.

Ettore was inspecting the small hole where Hector had found the stone.

"Good work," he said. "You didn't disturb anything more than what you had to. What made you dig it up, anyway?"

Hector didn't want to say he'd seen it shining. That must have been a trick of the light. So he just said, "It looked too round to be a regular rock." He hoped that Ettore wouldn't be angry with him for not calling him when he found "something interesting," but the archaeologist didn't seem to care. Maybe it was because he had already decided that the eye was modern.

Ettore nodded. "I think you understand how we work, now. Susanna said you may try in the trench when you showed me you could do the work. Would you like to?" He gestured behind him.

"Sure!" Hector said. There had to be more interesting

things than eye-shaped stones there. Maybe he'd find the tomb of a pharaoh. No, that was Egypt. Still, there had to be tombs here someplace. As Ettore said, the Etruscans didn't just throw dead bodies in the trash. Or not usually.

"I will be next to you," Ettore said. "Come on."

Ettore lowered himself into the trench and Hector followed. "Here." Ettore handed him a toothbrush and a small pick. "The dirt down here is different from what it is near the surface. Do like so." With the sharp end of the pick, he gently poked at the hard-packed earth, then brushed off what he had loosened. When he reached a lump of something that didn't crumble, he left it in its place and worked next to it, loosening more soil. He kept on until Hector could clearly see the hard object that now stuck out from the surrounding dirt. Ettore pulled it out and shrugged. "This time, just a rock. Next time—who knows?"

Hector held the tools awkwardly. The air was damp and thick in the pit, making it hard to breathe. It even smelled moldy. He prodded the dirt tentatively and nothing happened. "Don't be scared," Ettore said. "You need to hit it—bam!—to break it." So Hector poked harder and was rewarded by a shower of earth. "Good," Ettore said. "I'll work here next to you, so you can ask me if you have a question."

Hector poked and brushed, brushed and poked. Twice he thought he'd found something, but in both cases it was only a stone. "Don't worry," Ettore said when Hector showed him his finds. "There are surely potsherds down here."

"Potsherds?" Hector said.

"Or shards," Ettore said. "Pieces of pots. They might not be beautiful, but they are useful to us. We can use them to tell how old is what we find around them."

Hector was getting bored and thought of telling Ettore he'd had enough for the day. Then something sticking out a bit from the dirt wall caught his eye. It was hard to say what was different about that particular dark lump, but once he saw it, he couldn't stop looking at it.

"Can I dig over there?" he asked, pointing with his brush. Ettore glanced over, seemed not to notice anything unusual, and said, "Certainly." He told Hector some more about what was so important about pieces of pots, but Hector stopped paying attention, because this time he was certain he had found something. It was black, not reddish like the dirt or gray like stone, and it was smooth and shiny.

Ettore noticed his concentration and moved closer. A couple of times he seemed about to take the pick from Hector's hand, but instead he stopped and let Hector do the work himself. Hector felt his heart leap with excitement as he realized that what he was slowly revealing to the dim light inside the trench was a shiny piece of pottery, curved and smooth.

When the sherd was finally freed from the surrounding dirt, Hector gently pried it out and turned it over in his hands. "Here," Ettore said and passed him a bowl of water. "Wash it off." Hector hesitated. "Come on," Ettore said. "It has survived rain and earthquakes. A little water won't hurt it." So Hector dunked the sherd in the water and swished it around.

The curved piece of clay was no larger than his hand, and a soft black. White letters, slanting downward, were painted all over it. Hector passed the sherd to Ettore.

"What does it say?" he asked. Ettore shook his head, glanced at the spot where Hector had found it, and wrote something in his notebook.

"Take it to Betsy—to your mother," he instructed. "Perhaps she can read it." Hector climbed out of the trench and ran to where his mother sat, now wearing her broad-brimmed hat as the sun climbed higher.

"Mom! Mom! Look what I found!" He held the piece of broken pot toward her.

"Heck, you're not supposed to be messing around in the trenches," his mother said, frowning up at him.

"He wasn't making a mess." Ettore had joined them. "He was helping, with Susi's permission and mine. And see? He made a discovery."

"Sorry," his mother said. "I just thought—never mind. Let me see." Hector gave her his find and leaned over as she scrutinized it.

"*You* found this, Heck?" He nodded. "I'm impressed," she said. "There are some whole words here. Look." By that time a small crowd had gathered. A pot with writing on it must be more unusual than he had thought.

"Something about *zusleva*," she murmured. "That's 'offering,' or 'sacrifice.' Then *fanu*—that's 'sanctuary,' or 'temple.' Then the same word three times: *clan, clan, clan.* 'Son, son, son.'" She shook her head. "I wish there were more—it's impossible to tell what it means just from these few words. There's no way to know what they're talking about." She groped for her pen and pad and carefully copied the letters from the sherd.

One of the archaeologists glanced at his watch and said something, and they started to drift back to their trenches and pack up their tools. A lot of them said "congratulations" and "good job" to Hector as they went past, and he flushed with pleasure.

"Wow, it's late," his mother said. "Lunchtime." She handed the sherd to one of the archaeologists, who carried it to the shed.

"Good work," Ettore told him. "You hungry?"

"Starving," Hector said. "What time is it?"

"Almost one o'clock," Ettore answered. "Come on." Hector picked up his tools, and as they passed the shed, he put them back on the shelf. Then he trotted after Ettore, who was now talking with another archaeologist.

Hector was starting to feel sleepy again, and the heat of the afternoon wasn't helping any. He slowed down to follow the adults through the narrow stone arch, hoping he wasn't tagging along too closely, looking like a little kid who had to hang out with the grown-ups. But on the other hand, he didn't want to get separated from the rest of them. He had no idea where they were going.

As the shade of the wall hit him, Hector glanced up and blinked. He shook his head and looked again, but he hadn't been mistaken. Squatting on the edge of the enormous gray rock that made up the right-hand side of the arch was a boy in a long white shirt, looking solemnly down at Hector, his hand raised in greeting.

5

Hector's hand went up involuntarily—not to return the greeting but to shield his eyes from the sight of the boy. He gave Hector a queasy feeling. How did he get up on top of that arch? What was he doing there? And why were the others ignoring him? Hector broke into a trot.

His mother was waiting for him at a bend in the road. She smiled and pointed into a doorway, then went inside before he could speak to her.

The people from the dig were seated at long tables, like in a cafeteria. His mother patted the plastic chair next to her, and he slid into it. His hunger was replaced by shyness at having to eat in front of these people he didn't know, who were speaking all sorts of languages. He took a bite of bread. It was disappointing after the delicious roll of that morning.

Who was that boy? he opened his mouth to ask, but then his mother also bit into the bread. "Ah, tasteless Tuscan," she said.

"It is *not* tasteless," Ettore said. "It absorbs the taste of the other foods."

"Are you still litigating about that?" Susanna asked.

"Arguing," said his mother.

"*Eh già*," Susanna said, slapping her own forehead lightly with her open palm. "I will never remember. Are you still arguing about that? Twenty years ago you insulted the bread of Toscana, Betsy, and you defended it, Ettore. You also cited Dante."

"*Tu proverai si come sa di sale lo pane altrui*," Ettore said, his hand on his chest and his eyes rolling up to the ceiling. Hector put down his bread next to his plate. Didn't anyone even care that he couldn't understand Italian?

"Dante was wrong and you're wrong," Hector's mother said, but with a laugh in her voice.

"Dante? *Wrong?*" Ettore pretended to faint.

A white-uniformed woman plunked a heavy bowl down in front of Hector. In it was clear brown soup with a few noodles. He tasted the broth. It looked plain, but it was delicious, and he had no trouble finishing the bowlful. He felt his appetite come bounding back. *This will never be enough*, he thought.

"Show your mother what else you found today," Ettore said. Hector pulled the eye out of his pocket. It flashed as his mother took it, but she didn't seem to notice. She turned it over in her hand until the blue eye was staring up at her.

"So it's not Etruscan?" she asked, as she handed it back to Hector.

"Unfortunately, no," Ettore said, and he gave Hector a sympathetic grimace. "Some Greek tourist must have dropped it. You know they carry these things against the *malocchio*—the bad eye."

"*Evil* eye," she said. "How do you know it's not ancient?"

"Too superficial," Ettore said.

"Shallow," she corrected. "Anyway, I thought that sometimes hard things could work their way up to the surface."

Ettore shrugged. "It's not usual."

"Well, it's not like you can carbon-date stone," Hector's mother said as he put the eye back in his pocket. It felt strangely heavy, and he shifted on the hard seat.

One of the uniformed women took away Hector's empty soup bowl. He looked after it longingly as his stomach rumbled.

"*C'hai ancora fame?*" the woman asked, with a gap-toothed grin. He looked at his mother.

"She wants to know if you're still hungry," she translated.

"*Sì*," Hector said. The woman said something rapidly to his mother.

"She says not to worry, that there's more coming."

"*Grazie*," Hector said, and he was rewarded with another smile. And in a moment the woman came back, carrying one plate heaped with chicken and another with french fries. A second woman brought a big bowl of salad.

Everything was so good that Hector didn't realize how much he'd eaten until he saw the pile of chicken bones on his plate. They reminded him of the bones in the trench. Fortunately, one of the women whisked his plate away and replaced it with a cardboard container of ice cream. As he scraped out the last of it, she reappeared and put another one in front of him, patting him on the shoulder. "*Bravo!*" she said. It was nice to be congratulated for eating a lot when you were hungry. And for accidentally finding a potsherd with writing on it.

Or was it really an accident? Ettore, an experienced archaeologist, hadn't seen anything unusual about that sherd before Hector had dug it out. Maybe he had been led to it somehow.

He shook his head. That was ridiculous. You can't be led to a broken pot.

The room was half empty by now. Susanna had left before the ice cream arrived. Ettore was stretching and yawning. "See you this afternoon," he said.

"What time do you start up again?" Hector's mother asked.

"About four o'clock," he said. "It isn't cool before then."

"Aren't we going back to the dig?" Hector asked.

"Not now," Ettore said. "It's too hot out there, especially in the trenches. We all take a nap for a few hours and then go back to work after the hour of Pan."

At the word *nap* Hector suddenly felt as though someone had glued a weight to his eyelids. How could he be sleepy? It was only about seven o'clock in the morning at home. His body clock must be totally screwed up.

"What do you mean, 'the hour of Pan'?" his mother asked.

"You don't know?" Ettore asked. Hector and his mother shook their heads. "During the hot part of the day is when the clever little god Pan used to come out and play his pipes and make his strange shout. When the animals heard it, they would run around and be crazy. That's why we call being scared, being in a *panico*—a panic—from the name of Pan."

"Do you believe that story?" Hector asked.

Ettore looked into his eyes. "I have never seen Pan myself," he said. "But just because I haven't seen something, this doesn't mean it isn't there, right?"

"Right," Hector said.

"Sometimes when it's hot in the field, and quiet, it's almost like you can feel something. It's as if all the different times that people have lived here are together at once." Ettore shook his head and laughed. "I know—I sound crazy, right? But maybe this is why I became an archaeologist. I want to know my ancestors, the people who used to live here." He yawned again and left.

His yawn made Hector yawn so long and hard that it felt like his jaw was going to pop.

His mother put her hand on his. "I know how you feel," she said. "I want to crawl into bed and sleep for twenty-four hours. But it's really best if you keep awake. If you fall asleep now you won't wake up for ages and it will just take longer to get on Italian time."

"So I'll go watch TV," he said. She shook her head.

"The fastest way to go to sleep is to watch TV in a language you don't know," she said. "Take it from one who's been there. I'm going to try to figure out the rest of the words on that sherd. Why don't you take a walk or something? Just don't dig without someone there to supervise you."

Hector didn't need convincing. The last thing he wanted was to sleep—and dream—again. He decided to walk down to the dig.

The whole town seemed to be asleep. On the walk down all he heard was the faint whirr of some engine, and the noise just made him drowsier. He walked around the little hill near the excavation. It had gotten really hot. He wanted to go look at the olive trees but found that they were farther away than they appeared, so he sat down in the shade of a big rock and pulled off his shoes and socks, letting the air dry his sweaty feet. Someone had spray-painted ANGELA TI ADORO on the boulder in bright red. A small stream came down from the hill and flowed almost silently next to him, disappearing into the olive grove.

It was so quiet. Everything seemed to be waiting out

the hour of Pan. Some insects buzzed, but that and the gurgle of the stream were all he heard. He leaned back against the rock. When he closed his eyes, he whirled with sleepiness, so he sat up straighter and shook his head.

He felt vaguely uneasy. It must be Ettore's silly story about the hour of Pan. But despite his feeling of apprehension, he was having a hard time keeping his eyes open. *Why didn't anyone tell me jet lag felt so bad?* he thought. *It's like you're separated from your body.* His eyelids grew even heavier. *I'll just close them for a minute,* he told himself as once again the image of a spinning globe filled his mind.

He was in a red and brown landscape. The sky was so bright it burned his eyes, and the dry air pierced his nostrils. Gritty dust parched his throat.

"Time doesn't work like that," someone said behind him, but this time it wasn't his mother. It was a young voice, a boy's voice. Hector twisted his head, but whoever had spoken kept moving out of sight.

"Who are you?" Hector asked, still trying to catch a glimpse of the speaker.

There was no answer.

"*What* are you?"

"Rashna," came the reply.

"Why are you haunting me?" he cried out, and his own voice woke him up.

6

Okay, that was enough. He'd had two nightmares in one day, and it wasn't even night yet. He had to convince his mother to take him home. If she wanted to stay here with her Italian friends, fine. He could fly back by himself. Lots of people his age did it. He pictured the rest of the summer, with friends to hang out with, long lazy days at the lake, no bossy sister to tell him that it was her turn on the computer. He could stay up all night and sleep all day. No jet lag–induced nightmares. It would be great.

He might have to spend a lot of time on his own, though. Max was away at camp and Zach had moved to Pennsylvania as soon as school ended. Joaquin was spending the summer with his father in Costa Rica.

That was okay, though. Compared to having nightmares every time he closed his eyes, it would be better to go bike riding and swimming on his own.

Except his parents' rule was that you needed a buddy when you went swimming. And it looked like a buddy was exactly what he'd be missing. And his dad would say that he was too busy to go to the lake or bike riding with him and that he should have stayed in Italy.

He leaned back against the boulder and tried to ignore the prickling in his eyes that meant that tears were threatening. He rubbed the back of his hand against his eyelids and thought, *Stupid dust*.

Voices from the dig caught his attention. Cautiously he rose to his feet and leaned around the boulder to see who it was. It was some of the archaeologists from this morning, and it looked as if they were getting ready to get to work again. He walked the short distance back and looked into the trench where the bones had been found. But a tarp was laid over them and there was nothing to see.

Ettore appeared. "Oh, Hector, there you are," he said. "Betsy was looking for you."

"She told me to go for a walk," Hector said. Why did his mother treat him like a little kid who would get lost?

"I know, but that was more than two hours ago." Ettore pulled a cell phone from his pocket.

Two hours? Had he really slept for all that time? He shook his head, trying to clear it, as Ettore spoke into the phone.

"Betsy? *È qui. Dormiva.*" He laughed, said, "*Eh già. Ciao,*" and flipped the phone shut.

"She says you're good at sleeping," he said. "Come on. Let's give a look to the new trench." Before Hector could protest that there wasn't any point, since he was going to get his mother to send him home soon, Ettore hopped down into an opening in the earth that looked darker and fresher than the other holes. He held up a hand to help Hector in. *Honestly,* thought Hector, ignoring the offer of assistance as he hopped down after the man, *it's not like I'm a baby. I can jump a few feet.*

"Sorry," Ettore said, lowering his arm. "I keep forgetting you're eleven. Your mother sent me lots of pictures when you were a baby and I'm not used to you being big."

"That's okay," Hector said. "I'm short for my age, anyway." Now he couldn't say anything about leaving Italy. Ettore would think he was acting like a little kid with hurt feelings.

"We just opened this trench last week," Ettore was saying. He poked a finger thoughtfully into the soil and rubbed the dust between his fingers. "There's something that interests me here. The grass above here was growing differently, and it made me think there might be something large under the ground. We have not dug very deeply yet, but I think that we may find a building."

"What kind of building?" Hector asked.

Ettore shrugged. "That much, I do not know," he said. "But we are in the center of the city, so it could be something important. Shall we find out?"

"Sure!" Hector said. Talking to his mom about the nightmares could wait. She hadn't yet reappeared at the dig, anyway, and he didn't feel like trekking all the way back up that steep hill to find her. Maybe that evening. If lunch was that good, he couldn't wait to see what they'd serve for dinner.

"Where are your tools?" Ettore asked.

"*Eh già*," Hector said as he hoisted himself out of the trench again, earning a grin from Ettore.

When he returned, clutching his collection of picks and brushes, Ettore was already at work. He moved over to make room for Hector, and for an hour or so they worked in companionable silence. Hector's mother poked her head in and said something about him being a sleepyhead, but Hector just answered her briefly and kept on working. Scrape, poke, brush, shake. It could have gotten monotonous, but since there was always the chance that something might turn up, the time passed quickly.

When they put down their tools and hoisted themselves out of the trench, a breeze had sprung up and the air was cooler. Ettore glanced at the sky.

"Perhaps it will rain," he said. Hector nodded cautiously, his neck too stiff from bending close to the trench wall to allow him to look up. He wiped his tools with the cloth that Ettore passed him and slid them back in their pouch.

As Ettore stopped to talk with the freckled-faced archaeologist, Hector joined the stream of people heading up the slope to the opening in the city wall.

"What do you think they'll have for dinner?" he asked his mother as she fell into step next to him.

"Oh, some kind of pasta first," she answered. "And then, who knows? Why, are you hungry?"

"Starving," he said, and she laughed.

"As usual. Watch out, or we'll have to pay for two seats for you when we go back in August."

"Speaking about going back—" he started, but she just went on as though he hadn't said anything.

"And anyway, first a shower, then dinner," she said. "You're filthy, and dinner isn't for another half hour." She yawned. "What a long afternoon."

"It went fast for me," he said.

"Well, time's relative," she observed. "It's not fair that it should go slower when you're bored, but that's the way it is. Why was it such a good afternoon, anyway? Did you find something else?"

"No."

"Yes, we did." Ettore had caught up with them. "We found discolorations in the soil that I think will show that the earth has been moved. Perhaps this is because something large was built there."

"Like a temple," Hector said, passing through the arch. He kept his eyes on the ground, not knowing why the thought of seeing that boy again made him so uneasy.

"I hope," Ettore said. "A temple would be magnificent."

"I didn't see any discolorations," Hector said.

"You need some experience, and you need to know how to see it," Ettore said. "I will show you tomorrow."

Dinner started with pasta, as his mother had predicted. Long strands of something like spaghetti, but flat, were served in a creamy cheese sauce, followed by pork chops and salad. There was more of that tasteless bread, and apples for dessert. They were small and dull-colored but so sweet and juicy that Hector ate three of them.

That must be why he was having so much trouble falling asleep, he thought an hour later as he flopped over on his narrow bed. He was wide awake and uncomfortably full. And the longer he lay there, the more alert he felt. He turned over again.

Well, no wonder he couldn't sleep, with that bright light shining from his bedside table. Funny he hadn't noticed it before. But where was it coming from? It wasn't his clock; the red numbers that showed 11:46 and then 11:47 were dim and familiar. Had someone left a flashlight in a drawer and he had somehow turned it on by accident? He groped to find it and switch it off. Maybe then he could get some sleep.

But there was no drawer in the table. He picked up his summer reading book, which he'd halfheartedly started at bedtime, and the light that shot out at him from under it made him drop the book and cover his eyes.

After a moment, when his heart had stopped thumping and when he thought his eyes must have adjusted to the glare, he squinted out from behind his fingers.

It was coming from that Greek good-luck piece, or whatever it was. Maybe it was one of those glow-in-the-dark things.

But no. He had seen glow-in-the-dark toys before and their light was nothing like this. It was always pale green and very dim. This was pure white and so bright that he still couldn't look directly at it. With his head half turned away, he wrapped his hand around the stone, hoping to muffle its glare with his fingers. As he did so, his stomach lurched with a feeling of panic.

What is with *this crazy thing?* he thought. Maybe it was radioactive. He made up his mind to show it to his mother. Surely she would have some logical explanation. He rose to his feet, the light streaming from between his fingers, and made his way out the bedroom door, then toward his mother's room.

Instantly, the light went out. Hector's eyes had been so dazzled that now he felt blind in the dark hallway, and he put his hand on the rail to steady himself. Now what? He couldn't go to his mother with this cold, dark stone and tell her that it had been glowing. She'd say he'd been dreaming and send him back to bed. Then she'd tell everybody about it in the morning and they'd all have a good laugh at him. No thanks.

He tightened his hand on the railing. Was it his imagination, or did the light come back faintly when he turned toward the stairs? Experimentally, he faced his mother's bedroom. The eye was cold and heavy and as dark as a piece of ordinary rock. He turned toward Susanna's room. No change. He took a step toward the head of the stairs.

It was unmistakable. A faint white glow came from the eye. He took a step down and it grew slightly stronger. With each step, it became brighter.

At the foot of the stairs, he turned toward the kitchen. The light dimmed until it was almost out. Then he faced the front door and the glow came back. He reached out a hand and turned the knob, and he could have sworn that the eye shimmered as though with joy.

Hector stepped out into the night air. It was cool, especially since he was wearing nothing but boxers. Not a sound disturbed the peace of the streets. He started down the hill, keeping his gaze fixed on the eye in his hand, watching it grow brighter and brighter. When the light dimmed, he knew he had headed in the wrong direction, and so he turned until it brightened again.

Almost before Hector knew it, he was standing at the edge of the dig. *That must be what it wants*, he thought. *I have to put it back where I dug it up*. So he turned away and took a step toward the spot by the tree where he'd found the eye-shaped stone that morning.

Instantly, the light went out.

What did it want? He turned slowly until he saw the glow on his palm, then took a step, and then another. He stumbled forward, over mounds of earth and tree roots and stones. When the light stayed steadily bright, he kept going in the same direction. When it grew dim, he turned until it shone again. It was like playing a game of hot-and-cold at a little kid's birthday party.

He wasn't paying attention to where he was going. The moon came out from behind a cloud, casting a cool light on the ground in front of him, just as the eye flashed a single triumphant ray and then went out.

Hector jerked himself backward just in time. If he had stepped forward instead, he would have pitched headfirst into a trench. And not just any trench. The trench where Ettore had found the human bones.

1

Hector froze and swallowed hard. Why had the eye led him here? What did it want him to do? And why hadn't he noticed before how much the trenches looked like open graves, yawning blackly in the moonlight?

"What do you want?" he asked. "Do you want me to go in there?" The sound of his own voice rang strangely in the stillness. At that moment, the moon slid behind another cloud. The wind picked up, and the leaves moving in the breeze sounded like rain. Then he realized that it *was* rain, and it was coming down pretty hard.

Now what? He could hardly see to find his way back in the downpour, and the path into town would be too slick to walk on. He glanced into the trench, made up his mind, and slid cautiously down into it. He plastered himself against the side farthest away from the bones and pulled the tarp over his head.

It didn't help much. Water ran down the sides of the trench and pooled beneath him. The air was thick under the waterproof covering. The smell of mud and of something heavier, thicker, was inescapable.

Stupid eye, Hector thought. *If only I hadn't found it. I'd be in my bed right now, and dry.* He shifted his weight uncomfortably, hearing a squelch from every part of his body that touched the earth. He leaned back against the wall of the trench and tried to get comfortable, hugging his knees to his chest.

The people were still looking toward the columned building, and when the door flew open, everyone standing near it jumped back as though startled.

"What is it?" Hector asked, but no one seemed to hear him. He cleared his throat and tried again, louder. "What's in there?" Nobody paid him the least attention.

Then a shadow moved in the doorway of the building, and everyone leaned forward.

It was only a boy. He was a little smaller than Hector, with long black hair that fell forward, covering most of his face. He was dressed in a kind of T-shirt that fell to the middle of his thighs. He wore a pouch of what looked like leather on a cord around his neck. He was barefoot. As he hesitated in the doorway, someone must have pushed him from behind. He stumbled down the short stairway and fell heavily to his knees. He couldn't break his fall, Hector realized, because his arms were tied behind him.

Nobody stepped forward to help the boy. Nobody said anything to him, either, although a low buzz of voices arose as people turned to each other and murmured.

The boy struggled to his feet and looked behind him toward the building. He said something in a pleading tone. There was no answer, and he turned his tear-stained face toward the crowd. He scanned it as though looking for someone or something.

The boy's face turned in Hector's direction, and Hector shuddered as a wave of déjà vu washed over him again. This time it didn't slip away. Hector knew that boy, knew the face that was revealed when the shiny hair fell back to show the dark skin, the long, bright eyes.

It was the boy he had seen on the wall, the one who had waved casually at Hector as he walked up toward the town.

The boy gave a start, and his large eyes widened as though in surprise or in recognition.

"It's you!" he cried hoarsely. "I knew you'd come! You must help me! I'm almost out of time!"

"How?" Hector asked, but at the sound of his own voice, the déjà vu started to fade, and the dream with it. As he felt himself slide from the hot, dry square full of murmuring people into the mud and the air under the tarp, which was warm and wet with his breath, the boy's voice, fading rapidly, said, "You have it . . . I know you have it . . . Use it to come back . . ." And then there was silence.

The rain had stopped. Hector pulled the tarp away from his head, and the cool night air washed over him, lifting the damp hair off his forehead. He pushed back his bangs with trembling fingers and got shakily to his feet. *It was a dream*, he told himself firmly. *Just a dream, and now it's over.* But what did that boy mean by being almost out of time? *Just a dream*, he reminded himself, as he searched for a toehold in the packed earth. If his mother woke up and noticed he was missing, his life wouldn't be worth living.

Clouds still covered the moon, and the wind was chilly. He hoisted himself out and, clutching the eye-stone, picked his way around the trenches. He was starting to breathe more easily. Only a few trenches lay between him and the shed and then the path up the hill. But something grabbed his ankle, and with a sickening lurch, he fell face forward into nothingness.

He hit the ground almost right away. What had tripped him up, he realized even as he fell, was not some ghostly hand but one of the strings stretched across the edge of a trench. And this one was fairly shallow, so although he was shaken from the fall, he didn't think he was hurt. It must be the trench he and Ettore had started earlier that day, the one that Ettore thought would lead them to a temple. All the others were much deeper.

He had dislodged a lot of clumps of soggy dirt in his fall. They were cold and scratchy, and they fell apart when he stepped on them.

More cautiously this time, he made his way through the dig and onto the path that led through the stone arch. The flat rocks that made up the path were as slick as if they had been oiled. He walked slowly and carefully but still stumbled a few times. He shivered as the cold air bit into his wet skin. It started to rain again and soon it was pouring hard. The mud streamed off him until he was as clean as if he had just come out of the shower, with water plastering his hair to his head and running into his eyes and ears.

Standing in his small bedroom, he peeled off his sodden boxers, dropping them next to his bed. He slid between the rough sheets, which felt comfortably warm and real.

Slowly his shivering ceased and he started to feel deliciously drowsy. He had put the eye-rock on his bedside table, but now it cast no light. *Maybe it's tired too*, he thought nonsensically as he felt himself slip into a dreamless sleep.

When he woke, Hector could tell that the house was empty. Bright light squeezed through the cracks of the wooden shutters, which someone must have closed while he slept. He sat up, his mouth dry and his belly aching with hunger. And why did he have a nagging feeling of dread?

Then last night's dream came back to him. Of all the dreams he'd had since arriving in Italy, that one was the weirdest: a light coming from that Greek eye, leading him down to the dig, and then into the trench. He shook his head. Where had *that* come from? Because surely it had all been a dream. There was no way he would have gone wandering around a strange town in Italy, or anywhere else, in the middle of the night. Especially wearing nothing but a pair of old boxers.

The dream had probably come from the way the sun had reflected off the eye-stone when he'd found it the day before. In the way dreams happen, that reflection had twisted around into a light that sent him a message. The creepiness of those bones had somehow worked their way into the dream, and he was probably remembering the way he'd nearly fallen into the trench earlier but was caught by Ettore, and that's why he had dreamed about actually falling into one.

But it had been so vivid. He could still feel the cold stones under his bare feet as he walked first down, then up, the hill. He still felt the shock of tripping over the string and tumbling into the new trench. It was as real as if it had actually happened.

His boxers lay crumpled on the floor next to his bed. As he picked them up to toss them into the wicker laundry basket, they felt a little damp from lying on the cold stone floor all night.

Or from getting soaked in a midnight rain?

Ridiculous, he thought. *That was just a dream.* And he ran down the stairs.

A note in the kitchen read, "Bread on the counter, juice in the fridge. Come down to the dig when you've eaten. Mom."

It was the first time Hector had been alone in the house. The silence and the lack of supervision were relaxing. Now that there was nobody to tell him he had to eat at the table, he took his roll, spread with butter and strawberry jam, into the small living room. He watched music videos while he ate. He eyed the computer longingly, but his mother had threatened him with all sorts of consequences if he touched it. It was for Susi's work and it was ancient, anyway. He doubted that the connection was fast enough to make instant messaging possible. His mother had said he should write letters to his friends, but he didn't think it was worth explaining to her how stupid that would be, so he let it drop.

It felt late, somehow, when he went back upstairs to put on his shoes and brush his teeth.

As he was about to start down the stairs again, he hesitated and glanced back into his room. The stone lay on his bedside table, its blue and black eye facing away from him. It looked like a golf ball, cold and lifeless and inert.

So why did he feel as if he had to take it with him?

This was silly. He took a step down the stairs and paused again. *Oh, all right*, he thought. In his room, he picked up the stone and jammed it into his shorts pocket. Then he took off for the dig. It looked like it was already afternoon, or at least late morning, and who knew what had been turned up in the hours he'd wasted, first by sleeping and then by taking so long over breakfast?

When he got to the excavation, he thought at first that the archaeologists were back in the village taking their afternoon break. Where was everyone? Then he saw a group clustered around the trench where he and Ettore had been working the day before, the one that he'd dreamed about falling into last night. Something important must have happened for them all to be there instead of scraping dirt in their own areas.

It was impossible to see past all the bodies crowded around the edge of the trench. Hector felt awkward trying to push his way through, and he still didn't know which of the archaeologists spoke English, so he hovered on the edge until one woman moved aside to say something to the man next to her. He took advantage of the temporary gap to squeeze through.

Susanna and his mother squatted at one end of the trench. His mother was pointing at the wall of the trench while Susanna looked as though she was going to burst with curiosity or excitement. Ettore, behind them, leaned forward and tried to look over Susanna's shoulder. He glanced up and saw Hector.

"You slept too much!" Ettore called over the babble. "Something of interest is here. Can you see?"

"No," Hector answered. "What is it? Another sherd?"

"Better than a sherd," Ettore said. He stepped out and brushed the damp earth from his hands. "They won't let me near it anyway," he said, glancing at the two women, whose noses were practically pressed against the earth.

"What did you find?" Hector asked.

"A part of a wall, I think," he said. "A strange thing happened last night. It rained, did you know?" Hector nodded. "And in the darkness, an animal—a dog, probably—fell into the trench. When he fell, he broke the side we had dug. Large pieces of dirt came off and uncovered something flat and red. I think it is an *affresco*—a painted wall."

Hector nodded again and swallowed. A dog had fallen into the trench? The same trench that he'd dreamed about falling into last night?

"How do you know it was a dog?"

"A dog?" Ettore looked puzzled. "Oh, you mean what fell in the trench? There's not much other animals here. It was either a dog or a person, and I don't think many people like to go out at night in the rain."

An exclamation from inside the trench made them both look in that direction. Susanna had brushed away more dirt, and even from where they stood they could see that a picture was starting to emerge.

"What is it?" Ettore asked. The two women made no answer.

"Mom!" Hector said, the urgency in his own voice startling him. "What did you find?"

"Well," his mother said, "it's a little hard to tell just yet."

"Come on, Betsy," Ettore said. "Why then did you say 'Wow!'?"

"Because," Susanna broke in, "because we can't yet be certain, but it looks like there is a picture here that will answer some questions. A picture of a sacrifice."

8

A babble of voices greeted this news.

"A sacrifice?" Hector asked, but nobody seemed to hear him. His heart was pounding. He touched Ettore's arm. "How can they tell it's a sacrifice?"

"The priests wore special clothes during rituals," Ettore explained as he jumped back into the trench. He looked up at Hector. "And they carried a knife to cut the throat of what they were sacrificing. Perhaps there is something like that in this picture."

"What did they sacrifice?" Hector asked, but Ettore's attention was completely on the wall painting by now, and he didn't answer.

Hector clenched his fists. *Why* wouldn't anyone listen to him? Why couldn't they tell him what was going on? He might as well be invisible. People were crowding even closer to look into the trench, and he was pushed away.

Well, fine. If they weren't going to let him look, he wouldn't try. He walked away from the dig, taking a bottle of water out of the cooler as he passed it. He settled against the boulder a little way down the path. The small amount of shade wasn't quite enough to shield him from the blazing sun. It was better than nothing, though. He drew his feet up close to him and rested his chin on his knees.

The stone in his pocket dug into his hip. He straightened out his right leg and pulled out the eye. He was glad he hadn't tossed it away. It was the first thing he'd found on the dig, and even if it wasn't Etruscan, it was still pretty cool. He rolled it over in his hand until the blue part was gazing blankly up at him.

Maybe someday he would become an archaeologist and dig up something amazing, and the eye would go on display as Dr. Hector Fellowes's first find. Or maybe he'd wind up being a plumber, and this eye would be the only memory he'd have of his summer as an archaeologist. In either case, he was going to hold on to it.

Sometimes he envied his parents. There was no mystery left for them. They already knew what they were going to do with their lives, because they were doing it. They were married and living in Tennessee, where his father wrote screenplays that nobody produced and his mother taught Greek and Latin to college students. How would he wind up?

I wish this eye was a crystal ball, he thought. He must have spoken out loud, because somebody answered him.

"I can't help you see the future," the voice said. "But I can take you to the past."

He whipped his head around to see who was talking. Nobody. He must be imagining things again. He leaned back against the rock, trailing his fingers in the dirt, which was already dry after last night's downpour. The soft dust felt almost cool. He let his eyes half close, and the shimmering of the land in the sunshine grew even more pronounced.

He realized that once again he wasn't hearing anything—no birds, not a squirrel. None of the stray dogs he'd seen in the village seemed to want to come out into the heat. He must be too far from the dig to hear the chatter of the archaeologists.

It wasn't completely silent, though. The stream made a small rippling sound. And there must be a house on the other side of the hill, or behind some trees, because once again he heard the small sound of a stringed instrument. It sounded as if someone was practicing the guitar, but he couldn't see where it was coming from. The music was high and sweet and oddly unsettling. He leaned back and listened, feeling like it was pulling him, tugging him to someplace far away. It felt so delicious that he allowed himself to be pulled. *Just for a minute*, he thought as he let himself drift.

He was jolted back into alertness by a movement in the trees. *A dog or something*, he thought. But he didn't hear anything, and surely a dog would make some noise.

It must have been his imagination, he decided. Then he saw it again. Now it looked like someone was walking toward him. He sat still in the shadow of the rock, hoping whoever it was would go away. He didn't feel like making the effort to talk to anyone, especially if they didn't speak English. But the shape kept moving toward him.

As the figure approached, Hector could see that it was a boy with straight black hair. He sat up taller and squinted. The boy's clothes were weird—some sort of long white shirt and a pouch hanging around his neck that flopped on his chest as he walked. He looked familiar. Had Hector seen him in the town? No, he hadn't seen anyone there near his age except for some of the archaeologists. This kid couldn't be an archaeologist. Then it came to him. This was the boy who had been sitting on top of the arch, who had later shown up in his dream. It was a little embarrassing to see a stranger he had dreamed about, even though there was no way the other boy would know about that.

The boy walked up without speaking and sat down by the stream. He fixed his dark eyes on Hector, his thin brown arms wrapped around his shins. He looked so cool in that robe that Hector felt fussy and overdressed in his shorts with all their pockets, his shoes with multiple laces, his striped shirt.

The boy sat in silence, still looking at Hector with large, unblinking eyes. Hector cleared his throat. He felt like he had to say something, but before he could speak, the other boy said, "I can't take you to the future. But I can take you to the past."

"What?" Hector asked, startled.

"You wanted to see the future," the boy said. "I can't take you there. But I can take you to the past."

This must be another dream, Hector thought. *But it feels so real*. As real as that dream about the midnight walk to the dig, and falling into the trench.

"Who are you?" Hector asked.

"Arath," said the boy.

"What kind of name is that? German?"

"No," the boy answered. "It's Rashna."

"Rashna?" Hector asked. "You mean like ancient Etruscan?" The boy nodded. "Why did your parents give you an Etruscan name?"

"Because I *am* Etruscan," the boy said matter-of-factly.

"But I thought the Etruscans died thousands of years ago?"

"Well, I lived here thousands of years ago. But I haven't died."

"You're nuts," Hector said nervously. "You can't be thousands of years old."

"Oh, no," the boy answered. "I'm twelve."

"Okay, fine," Hector muttered. If this was some kind of joke, he didn't want to play along. He stood up and brushed the dirt off the seat of his pants. Maybe the crowd around the trench had thinned and he could go back and see what they had been so excited about.

But as he turned, he caught sight of the valley. He must have fallen asleep, because now it was cool evening and the long shadows made everything look different.

But it was more than the change in light. Something was terribly wrong.

The dig—where was the dig? Where was the shed, and where were his mother and Ettore and Susanna?

Instead of the blue-jeaned and T-shirted Americans and Germans and Italians, small people with copper skin and long dark hair were walking in the flat area where the trenches should be. Hector swung around. The hill still rose above him, but the houses were gone, and a thick forest covered its steep slopes. Where there had been a crowded town splattered on its sides now there were just a few low buildings. He looked back down to where the dig should be, disbelief crowding every thought out of his mind. Instead of a silver-green olive grove in the distance, tall, dark trees now cast a heavy shadow. In place of the trench where he'd found the broken pot, there was a pile of wood scraps and pieces of pottery, and behind it stood a magnificent, colorful building with a double row of columns in front and an inhuman, brightly painted face glaring down from the peak of the roof. He had seen that building before, but that was in a dream—a dream where something terrible was happening to that same boy. But now there was no silent, waiting crowd, and the boy was sitting next to him, hands unbound, no tearstains on his cheeks.

Hector swallowed hard. "What's happening?" he whispered. "What did you do with them?"

The other boy didn't answer, but he, too, rose to his feet and watched the activity with his hands on his hips, a smile curling his mouth.

There were lots of people. The littler children were naked except for a pouch hanging around each of their necks, and the adults weren't wearing much either. Some were talking, some were repairing a wall, and two young men were wrestling and laughing as older men looked on and shouted what sounded like encouragement.

Arath turned to Hector. "Welcome to my home," he said softly.

9

For a moment, Hector could only stare and blink, his mouth hanging open. Then he managed to sputter, "Your— your *home*? What are you talking about? What have you done with all the people? And the dig? And my *mom*?" Without waiting for an answer he tore along the path down to where the dig should have been.

In a few seconds he was in the midst of all those dark-haired people. They strode past him as though they didn't see him. Two women came by, and one of them almost bumped into him.

"Hey!" he protested, backing up. She didn't pay any attention but said something to the little girl with her, who nodded and ran off to join a group of naked children playing with what looked like marbles or jacks in the dirt.

What was the matter with her? Was she deaf? Or just ignoring him?

Something was weird about the sunlight, but he couldn't figure it out. And then he saw. He had no shadow.

The boy—Arath—had caught up and stood panting next to him.

"What's going on?" Hector demanded. "How did you do this?"

"Do what?" Arath asked. The woman who had just passed by turned and looked at Arath curiously and then moved on.

"This," Hector said, pointing at the busy square, the bright building, the group of children squabbling over something. "How did you get all these buildings here? Is this some kind of hypnotism?"

"No, it's real," Arath said, but Hector shook his head.

"You hypnotized me," he said, panic making his voice thin. "Or I fell asleep against that rock. This is just another dream." He pinched his arm, but it made no difference. He slapped his own cheek. The sting brought tears to his eyes, yet he did not wake up leaning against the boulder on a hot afternoon, with that unsettling music playing someplace far away. He was still there, in that strange place on a cool evening, with the boy watching him with a strange smile, as people walked and played, not noticing him.

Fear exploded in his stomach, shooting a tingling sensation down to his fingers and toes. "There's something wrong with me. I'm seeing things. I must be going crazy."

"No, you're not," Arath said soothingly, but Hector was lost in his terror and hardly heard him.

"I'm going crazy," he repeated. "I've lost my mind."

Arath gripped him by both arms and dragged him, still babbling, back to where they had been standing before. He pulled Hector behind a tree, where they couldn't be seen from the square below.

"Stop," he commanded. Hector shut up and stood there panting. "I'll take you home now, but you have to come back later and help me. You must promise."

Hector nodded. "I promise," he croaked. He would agree to anything, as long as things went back to normal.

Arath said some strange words, and Hector felt something suddenly squeeze his rib cage. He gasped for breath and lurched as the ground under his feet became soft, like mud, and then soupier, like pudding. The world turned dark, then gray, then had no color at all, and it swirled around him. All Hector could see were those dark eyes, and all he could hear was that guttural chant.

Then the swirling stopped and the voice fell silent. The eyes disappeared. Something solid was under him, and he lay as though gravity had increased until it flattened him.

He stayed that way for a moment, his eyes closed. What if he were to see those long-haired people when he opened them? What if that brightly colored building was still right behind him, the young men wrestling playfully in the open area? Finally he sat up and looked around. He was alone, next to the spray-painted boulder. He could have kissed the graffiti.

It was a hot, slow afternoon. He could hear the faint

buzz of insects. The sun pierced through the dark leaves of the nearby trees, and on his left was the olive grove. Down to his right was a trench full of busy archaeologists. A trowel lay nearby and from up the hill he heard sounds of traffic, accompanied by the smell of diesel fumes, even at that distance. No temple, no forest, no dark-skinned, half-naked people.

And no Arath. Was he a dream after all? Had Hector fallen asleep against the rock and had another nightmare? But as his head cleared and he began to breathe normally again, a voice tickled his ear.

"You promised," it said. Hector whipped his head around but saw no one.

He got shakily to his feet and made his way down to the dig. There was his mother leaning against a tree, sound asleep with her Etruscan dictionary open on her lap. He had to tell her what had happened, although she would never believe it. In the bright sun, with all the normal activity going on, he could hardly believe it himself.

"Mom!" he said. No response. He tried again, a little louder. "Mom!" She groaned and opened her eyes a crack.

"Heck, let me sleep a little," she mumbled.

"I need to tell you something," he said.

"Just a little nap." She went back to sleep.

Well, so that was that. She wasn't going to listen to him. He might as well be invisible.

"What's wrong?" asked a voice behind him. It was

Ettore. "Are you sad, Hector?" He stopped talking when he saw that Hector's mother was asleep. He motioned to Hector to move away a little.

"Are you sad?" he asked once again. Hector hesitated. What could he say? That a boy had taken him back in time to an Etruscan village? Ettore would tell the others, and then they would laugh and say he'd been dreaming. So he just shook his head.

"You *look* sad," Ettore noted, his head on one side, considering Hector's face. Hector shrugged. "Are you missing your father and your sister?"

"No," Hector said. "I don't see much of them even when we're home."

"Your friends?"

To his surprise and embarrassment, Hector felt his face turn hot and his eyes sting with tears. He looked away so Ettore wouldn't see, but the man didn't appear to mind.

"It's too bad there are no other kids here," he said. "Shall I ask in the village and find out if there is someone who wants to play with you?"

"No," Hector said, so loudly that he startled himself. "I mean, no, thank you." Did Ettore think he was five years old and needed someone to *play* with?

"Okay," Ettore said. "Why not be an archaeologist for the summer, then? You are good at it, and you could be a help. Really," he added, as Hector hesitated. "I'm not saying that the way you say to a little boy, 'Oh, what a helper you are.' I mean it. You found the most important sherd of this summer, and I myself walked past that same piece a dozen of times without noticing it. What was it that made you want to dig it out, anyway?"

Hector said, "I don't know. It just looked different, somehow. Like it didn't belong."

"Good eye," Ettore said approvingly. "So, you want to be an apprentice archaeologist?"

Hector nodded. It was either that or watch the same music videos over and over again until they went home.

"*Bravo*," Ettore said. He took Hector to the shed and showed him the different implements the archaeologists used and his own most useful tool, a small notebook in which he carefully wrote down where each piece of pot, scrap of metal, and broken brick was found. This was the whole point of the dig, he explained. Sure, it would be great to find a beautiful statue or a pot of gold, but the things that excited archaeologists were usually small, and uninteresting to other people. A coin with the picture of a ruler whose dates historians knew, a vase shaped in a way that no one made until a certain time, a written text mentioning a historical event—these were the real treasures for archaeologists. Hector concentrated. What Ettore was saying helped keep him from thinking about what he'd seen that afternoon.

"When we study these things we learn about the

people who made them," Ettore explained. "It's like going back in time. These were our ancestors—not just mine, but yours too, since the Etruscans helped the culture of Rome take form, and the Romans went all over Europe, and the Europeans went all over America. If we know where we have come from, we understand *us* a little better. For example, if that building over there is a temple—" He stopped talking and shook his head ruefully.

Hector glanced up to see if a cloud had covered the sun, but no, the sky was still an unbroken, piercing blue. Then why had he felt a chill, deep enough to cause a shudder?

"It *is* a temple," he said without thinking, and then flushed.

"How do you know?" Ettore asked.

Hector shrugged. He couldn't say, "Because I saw it when it was whole." He wouldn't know how to explain it. And Ettore would tell him he'd been dreaming or think Hector was a baby playing make-believe.

"I just bet it is," he said lamely.

"I bet it is too," Ettore agreed. "But I won't be sure until I find more things."

"What kind of things?"

"I won't know until I find them. But temples usually had an altar. There might also be some holy objects. In a museum is a famous bronze model of a liver that an Etruscan priest used when he looked at the liver of a sacrificed animal to see the future, so he could know what the different shapes on it meant. If I found something like that . . ." His voice trailed off.

"You'd be famous," Hector said.

"I would be famous," Ettore agreed, and he laughed. "But more important is that the foundation that pays us would notice our dig and would give us more money. If we don't find something big soon, our money will run out. We're running out of time."

"And what would you and Susanna and everyone else do then?"

"I don't know," Ettore said shortly, as though he didn't want to talk about it. "I don't like to think of it. So hold your eyes open and find me a liver of bronze or a book of linen or a tomb with beautiful paintings, and I won't have to worry about it."

"I'll do my best," Hector said. It sounded like a big responsibility, and even though he hardly knew Ettore, he felt the urgency behind the man's joking words. If the dig closed, there would be no reason for his mother to stay and they could go home and he would have the rest of the summer there. But somehow that didn't seem so important anymore.

Besides, he'd had a strange feeling when he was helping Ettore before. It wasn't excitement and it wasn't curiosity. It was a kind of satisfaction, as if he was doing something he was *supposed* to be doing. Like scratching an itch. He made up his mind that if there were something to find here, he would find it. So after lunch he set to work.

He worked for what seemed like hours. It felt good to keep busy, because the heat was making him drowsy again, and the activity kept him focused. Also, this way he had something to think about other than that crazy kid.

His fingers were getting cramped, so he decided to take a break. He laid down his tools and hoisted himself out of the trench. His mother hadn't joined in the digging, but then she was there as a language expert, not as an archaeologist. She was sitting under a tree with the fat book open on her lap. He walked past a trench to get to her. Some of the diggers looked up at him as he passed, and they smiled. One said, *"Ciao!"* which he answered in Italian, earning him the usual grin.

"It's going to take them all summer to get anywhere if they just use those tiny tools," he told his mother.

"It would take a lot longer than one summer," she said. "They started this dig almost five years ago. But some parts are more dug out than others."

Hector flopped down next to her. He rolled over onto his back, looking up at the dark-green leaves. He wondered where that strange boy had gotten to.

"Mom?"

"What?"

"What happened to the Etruscans?"

"At first it was kind of like what happened to the American Indians when the Europeans came," she said, laying down her book. "The Romans killed most of the Etruscans and took their land. And then the ones who were left just blended in until after a while they weren't a separate group anymore. Their religion and traditions mixed with the Roman ones until you couldn't really tell which was which. Then their language got lost, mostly anyway."

"What do you mean, mostly?"

"There are some grave inscriptions in Etruscan, but all they say is that So-and-So, son of Such-and-Such, aged some number of years, lies here."

"Not too exciting," Hector said.

"No," his mother agreed. "That isn't quite all that we can read, of course. Once in a while, some small written text is found, but still, a lot of the words are unclear. It's very frustrating, like the Etruscans are trying to talk to us and we can't understand them. That's why a find like your sherd is so important. Anything we can discover with writing on it helps us to figure out a little bit more about them. Almost all their culture has been lost. The Romans weren't big on preserving other peoples' ways of life."

"So there couldn't be anyone around today who's really an Etruscan?"

"Well, some people here say they're Etruscans. Ettore, for one. But there was so much intermarriage for centuries and centuries that I doubt there's anyone alive today with only Etruscan blood. Why?"

"Oh, nothing," Hector mumbled, and he got up and went back to the trench. He worked until he could tell by the cooler air that it was getting late. When he hoisted himself out, he saw that everyone else was packing up too, and he joined the line of tired people heading up the hill to dinner.

Instead of the soup they'd had for lunch, dinner was spaghetti with meat and hardly any tomato sauce, and then thin slices of pale beef and some kind of stringy green vegetable that he didn't recognize. He saw the others pouring a few drops of vinegar on it, so he did too, and was surprised at how good it was.

As one of the ladies took his plate away, he suddenly felt as though he had been hit by a truck. All he could think about was crawling into that narrow little bed in Susanna's house. He looked at his watch. Eight o'clock Italian time, so it was early afternoon at home.

He realized that his mother and Ettore were watching him and laughing.

"What's so funny?" he asked.

"You," his mother said. "You look like you did when you were two years old and missed your nap. Come on. Let's go back to the house."

He stumbled up the uneven stones, dragged himself up the stairs, and pulled off his shoes. "You can skip brushing your teeth tonight," his mother said, but he heard her distantly, as though she were a TV in another room, and was asleep almost before he lay down.

He was in thick, swirling mist in a timeless in-between place. Somehow he could feel that he was not in the present and not in the past. Three figures stood before him, tall and beautiful and strange-looking, with pointy little smiles and huge, dark eyes. The man had broad shoulders and slim legs, and his hair fell in thick ropes down his bare back. The hair of the two women was bound tightly, and their long noses made their pale, thin faces appear very proud. One wore a long dress. The other had on a shorter skirt, and she carried weapons like a warrior.

"We have chosen you," their three voices said together, although their mouths didn't move.

Hector bowed. He didn't know what else to do, but this must have been correct, because they bowed back gravely. Then they spoke together again.

"We are eternal. We are not of this time, and we are not of that time."

"I am Uni, the earth, the mother," said the woman in the long dress. "I am life. I am eternal. I am beyond time."

"I am Tinia, the sky, the father," said the man. "I am strength. I am eternal. I am beyond time."

"I am Menrva, the mind, the daughter," said the woman with the helmet and spear. "I am thought. I am eternal. I am beyond time."

They looked at him in silence. Was he supposed to answer them? What could he say? "I am Hector"? But then they faded and the air cleared, and sound and smell and touch returned. Once again he found himself in that first dream-place: the open square, the temple, the crowd.

It wasn't exactly the same, though. This time, the sun was lower in the sky, and the people seemed more puzzled than anxious. Arath was there, kneeling with his head bowed, long dark hair falling forward, and his hands were bound behind him. Even without seeing his face, Hector recognized him this time.

Arath looked up then, his expression bleak. He caught sight of Hector and pleaded with him. "Please," he said hoarsely. "Please help me." But Hector felt frozen.

The boy's wrists were tied together in a way that looked painful, with the rope knotted very tightly. The man standing next to Arath said something sharply, and although Hector couldn't follow the words, he knew that Arath was asked who he was talking to. Arath nodded in Hector's direction and said something that must mean "that boy."

Another man, with a handsome but cruel face, strode over to Hector. It looked as if he was going to walk into Hector and knock him onto the hard earth, and Hector threw his hands out to keep him away. But the next instant the man passed through him as though he wasn't there. Hector felt a kind of shudder go through him, but that was all. He looked down at his body, his arms still stretched out to keep the man from running into him. Was the man some kind of ghost? Then Hector realized that he could see through his own feet to the dirt below. *He* was the ghost.

Before he had time to wonder at this, the man turned around to face Arath and said something harsh. Somehow Hector could understand him: He was saying that no one was there, that Arath was calling demons to do evil work. Arath protested, but his words were swallowed up in the shouts of the crowd. The cruel-looking man strode forward, grabbed Arath, and dragged him away, out of sight, into the temple.

The crowd fell silent, as though waiting. Suddenly screams and sobs burst from inside the temple. A woman in the crowd cried out and tried to push her way into the painted building, but other people held her back, speaking soothingly. She dropped to her knees and wailed, a high-pitched despairing sound that cut through Hector like a cold knife.

Hector suddenly found he could move, and he too tried to squeeze through the crowd to see what was happening, to make the screams stop, but everywhere he turned he was met with an angry, shouting face. He got confused and turned around to the point where he no longer knew where the temple was. And still the screams continued, making Hector's heart race as he imagined what might be going on. He tried to push against the wall of people, but his hands went through them. They didn't even react, and he realized that they couldn't feel him. He felt frustration building up in his chest until he wanted to explode with it.

The screams fell ominously silent. "Arath!" Hector cried. "Where are you? I'm trying to find you! I want to help!"

He was standing at the window in his little room in Sporfieri, clutching the cold stone sill. He rested his head against the window frame. What was he supposed to do? One thing was certain. He had to find Arath and do something to stop the dreams that were invading his sleep. He couldn't stand hearing the screams or seeing Arath's terrified face as he begged for help.

Hector shuddered and stared out the window at the strange, silvery color that the little light-brown houses took on by moonlight. They looked flimsy, almost as though he could see through them. He shook his head and looked again. It was strange what tricks the moonlight could play on you. A flicker of movement on the street directly beneath his window caught his eye, and he leaned forward. One of those stray dogs, probably.

But no. His heart skipped a beat as he recognized Arath, his face turned up. Even his tan skin looked oddly pale in the milky light. Arath didn't say anything, didn't make a single gesture with those expressive hands. He just looked up at Hector silently, his big, dark eyes shining even in the weak moonlight. Then he turned and walked away, down the stone streets toward the dig and the remains of the Etruscan village.

Hector just wanted to go back to bed and forget the whole thing, but he knew he couldn't. He pulled on the shorts he'd been wearing earlier and dug a warm sweater out of his suitcase. He slid his feet into his shoes, not bothering with socks, not bothering to tie the laces. Grateful for the rubber soles that made no noise on the hard floor, he slipped out of the house. He had lost sight of Arath but it didn't matter. He knew where to go.

No sounds came from the bakery. There were no sounds at all, in fact. The town looked dead. No lights shone out of the little houses, no motor scooters zoomed around corners. It was like he was wandering around on a huge stage before the play began. And just as in a play, the houses appeared made of sticks and cloth. They looked— well, *ghostly* was the only word he could think of. Like he could put his hand through them. Even though he knew he was being stupid, he patted one of them as he passed to reassure himself of its solidity.

His hand went through it. Not all the way through, but it was as though the house were made of sand and the grains shifted as he pushed on them. He yanked out his hand and stared at it. What was going on? He flexed his fingers. They worked. They were firm and warm. He broke into a trot. He had to catch up to Arath and find out what was wrong with the houses.

Hector slowed to a fast walk on the steep downhill slope, following the twists and turns of the road and taking the shortcut stairs whenever he saw any. He went through the final archway and found himself on the path leading to the archaeological site where he'd been digging—was it only that afternoon? It seemed like a hundred years ago. Or thousands of years in the future. He shook his head, trying to clear it.

As he approached the big rock near the dig, he heard a familiar voice.

"I knew you'd come."

10·

Hector didn't jump at the sound of that soft voice. He had been expecting it. He sat down heavily, leaning against the boulder. He looked up at the boy with the large eyes and white shirt that gleamed in the moonlight.

"So what's going on?" Hector asked. "Really. Who are you, and why do I keep dreaming about you?"

"I didn't do it," the boy—Arath—said. "*You* were the one who came to *my* dream. You said, 'Where are you? I'm trying to find you! I want to help!'" Hector shuddered as he heard his own words, the ones he had shouted in his dream. How could the boy know?

Was this still a dream? That would explain why things had felt so funny on the way down, why the solid rock wall seemed almost to melt under his fingers. All his senses were numb. The few sounds—Arath's voice, an owl, a dog barking in the distance—were fuzzy, like he was wearing headphones. He touched a branch. It didn't move, and although he could tell there was something between his fingers, it felt like he was wearing gloves.

Everything looked strange, too, like when he put on his father's glasses. When he stamped his foot, the ground felt different, like rubber instead of hard-packed earth. Was he sleepwalking? But he felt wide awake.

"It woke me up," Arath went on. "I was having a bad dream about someone beating me in the temple. Nobody would do that—you can't do something like that in the temple, especially to the son of the priest."

"Your father's a priest?" Arath nodded. "But I thought priests couldn't get married!"

"What?" Arath said. "Of course they can. They can have as many wives as they want. How else can you ensure that the priestly line will go on?"

"More than one wife?" Hector asked, bewildered.

"My father has three wives," Arath said, lifting his chin proudly. "My mother's the youngest, but she's the most important one. The other two never had any babies, and they're too old now. The elders said that since my father didn't have any sons, Cai—he's my father's cousin—would be the priest after him. They said there was a curse on my father. But then I was born, so Cai hates me. He knows that the only way he'll ever get to be priest is if I die.

"But my parents are worried because I'm their only child. My little sister died, and then three more times my mother thought she was going to have another one, but none of the babies got born alive. So the curse talk is starting again."

Arath's face puckered, and he paused.

"My father's scared," he went on after a minute. "I can tell. He says that the gods still tell him they love him and that he is their chosen one, but I don't know how long he'll keep believing that. And if something happens to me, then they'll know that the curse is true. And then Cai—" He stopped and shook his head, biting his lip as though trying not to cry.

Hector stood up again, feeling uncertain. "I—I'm sorry," he said lamely. He didn't know what else to say. Arath nodded without speaking. Hector went on. "I don't really know what you expect me to do."

The boy looked up at him. "I want you to help me."

"Help you?" Hector asked, truly mystified now. "How can I help you?"

"You can come to my village," Arath said. "You can do something from the spirit world to make Cai leave me alone. I've caught him looking at me with hatred in his eyes, and I don't know what he's planning to do, but I think he means to hurt me."

"But—" Hector started.

"I know what you're going to say," Arath interrupted him. "I know that when we went there before nobody could hear you or see you. I don't understand everything the sacred books say, but I think you would always be visible only to the person who took you to another time. You could tell me what to do, and I'll do it."

"That wasn't what I was going to say," Hector said. "I was going to say that it's impossible. You can't go backwards in time. What would happen if I went back in time and killed my own grandfather when he was a kid? Then I would never get born. But if I never was born, then I couldn't go back in time and kill my grandfather. And if I didn't kill my grandfather, then I'd get born, and then I could go back in time and kill him, which means I wouldn't get born, which means—"

"*Stop* it," Arath said. "Time doesn't work like that. If nobody can see you or hear you, you can't change things."

"So why should I go with you? If I can't change things, what's the point?"

"I already told you," Arath said. "If I take you, *I* can see you and hear you. You can tell me what to do and I'll do it. Then you can come back to your own time and we won't be in each other's dreams anymore."

"But if I tell you to do something it could still change the present, the same as if *I* were the one who did it. So what's the difference?"

Arath looked uncomfortable. His right hand strayed up to his chest and wrapped around the pouch that hung from his neck, as though for reassurance.

"I don't know for sure," he said. "But I think—I *think*—that if someone does something in his time, like me doing something in my time, it works out somehow— even if it's something you told me to do."

"But you're not sure."

Arath shook his head and clutched the pouch even more tightly.

"Who told you all this?" Hector asked. "Because you could ask them—"

"I read it in the holy books," Arath said. He looked guilty.

"So?" Hector asked.

"I read the holy books," the boy repeated.

"So what's wrong with that?"

"Only the priest is supposed to know how to read the holy books," Arath explained, as though talking to a small child. "He passes the knowledge on to his successor once the successor has had his manhood ceremony. I used to get bored during the rituals and would follow along with my eyes when he held the gold pointer under the words he was reading, and after a while I realized that I knew what he was going to say before he even got there. That meant I was reading." He stopped and looked at Hector, who realized that this was a kind of confession.

"Go on," he said.

"And then—" Arath hesitated, then seemed to gather up his courage. The next words came out in a rush. "And then, sometimes when I was supposed to be tending to the temple, I would take down the books and read them. I wanted to see if I could find some way of keeping myself safe from Cai. It's getting worse. I think he's planning something. And nobody is supposed to touch the sacred books but the priest. If you do—" He stopped talking and shivered.

"And did you?"

"Did I what?"

"Find something to keep you safe from Cai?"

The boy looked surprised. "Of course," he said. "I consulted them after my dream and learned how to find you here."

"Here?" Hector repeated.

"Here, in my time," the boy said. He made a sweeping motion with his arm. Hector followed the gesture and looked around him.

Dawn must be near. The sky was turning grayish pink, and the air was tinged with warmth. For a moment he thought that it was the strange light that was making everything look different.

Then he realized that it was not just the light. Once again everything had disappeared—the dig, the shed, the olive groves, even the houses on the hill.

11

"All right," Hector said. "Enough. I give up. How do you do it?"

Arath sighed impatiently. Even in the dim light, Hector could see that he was rolling his eyes.

This was just too much. Here he was in the middle of the night—or the early morning, whichever—with a kid who was dragging him around in time, and when he asked for an explanation, all he got was one of those sighs, like when your parents are about to explain something for what they claim is the hundredth time. It was infuriating.

Hector stood up. "Forget it," he said coldly. "I don't believe you." Of course he believed him. But he had to do something to get that smug look off the kid's face.

Arath jumped up. "Why not?" he asked angrily, his hands on his hips. "I'm telling you the truth! Look around you. Is this your world? Don't you even believe your own eyes?"

"Well," Hector demanded, "if you're an ancient Etruscan, how come you speak English? And why don't you come to me when there's anyone else around? Are you afraid someone will recognize you? And why me, anyway? If you need someone to help you, why not go to the police or one of the adults around here? What can *I* do?" he finished.

For a moment, Arath stood in silence. Then he dropped his hands by his sides.

"I don't know," he said miserably.

"You don't know how come you speak English?"

"Oh, I know *that*," he said. "After I learned how to read the sacred books, I used to go to the temple when no one else was there and read parts out loud. I wanted to learn the ritual words beforehand. You know, so my father would be impressed with how little time it took to teach me. And one time I was reading the words for how to do a prophecy—you do know what a prophecy is, don't you?"

"Seeing the future," Hector said. "I'm not as stupid as you think I am."

"I don't think you're stupid," Arath said earnestly. "Really, I don't. I just don't know what you know and what you don't know."

"Okay," Hector said. "I know what a prophecy is. Go on."

"Well, it said not to read the next part out loud, but I didn't know any other way to memorize it, so I did, and it must have been some kind of magic, because all of a sudden, instead of just *seeing* the future, I was *in* the future."

"How could you tell?"

"Lots of ways," Arath said. "It couldn't have been too far in the future, because I recognized the trees, but they were bigger than they should have been. I knew the houses, but some had cracks in them. Places that used to have forests were cleared. And then, then it was like I slipped, not on the ground, but in time, and I wound up back in my own place."

"So how did you learn English?"

"Oh, that," the boy said. "I just listened to people in the different times when I traveled to the future. I learned Latin and Tuscan and Italian, and in the last few centuries I've learned English and German and French. And a little Spanish."

Hector looked at the boy without speaking. It made sense in a weird kind of way.

"*¿Qué tal?*" Arath asked hopefully in Spanish. Hector didn't answer.

"How far in the future did you go that first time?" Hector asked, interested in spite of himself.

"I don't know," Arath said. "A few years, I guess. I mean, it was still my time, but I didn't recognize anybody. I tried to talk to people to find out when it was, but they couldn't hear me or see me. And then I was afraid that I wasn't going to be able to get home, so I prayed to my protectors," and he quickly touched the pouch hanging from his neck, "and they brought me home again."

"So why did you do it again?"

"Wouldn't you?"

Hector shrugged. "Not if I thought I couldn't get home."

"But I trusted my protectors." Again, his hand brushed the leather pouch. "I knew they would take care of me. And also, I knew that I would be pulled back to my own time even if I didn't do anything to make it happen."

"What do you mean, 'pulled'?" Hector asked.

"It's like—" the boy looked around and frowned. He focused on the stream. "It's like in the spring, when the stream is full. If you fall in, it takes you where it wants you to go, no matter how hard you try to stay in the same place. It's like that with time. When I go away from my own time, I have to fight to stay there. That's why I can't be with you for very long. And after a while, it wins. The farther away from my own time I travel, the harder it is to stay there. But when I want to get back in a hurry, before time pulls me away, I still pray to my protectors and they always take me home."

"What do you mean, 'protectors'?" Hector asked.

"Don't you have yours?" Hector shook his head. "What, you've had your manhood ceremony already?" Arath looked skeptical. "How old are you?"

"Eleven," Hector said. "Why?"

"They do the ceremony when you're *eleven*?" the boy asked.

"Look," Hector said. "You've got to stop talking in riddles. What's a manhood ceremony, and what are protectors?"

For an answer, Arath loosened the rawhide ties on the pouch hanging around his neck. His long fingers pulled out several objects—a tooth, a tiny gold lump that could have been meant to represent a person, and a round white stone with a blue eye set in it. He lined them up on his palm.

This can't be, Hector thought, and he dug into his own pocket. He pulled out the eye and held it next to Arath's.

The two rocks were remarkably similar. They had the same lightning-shaped crack radiating out from the blue center, only the crack in Hector's was deeper. Some fuzz from the leather pouch was stuck to Arath's, but otherwise they were identical.

"That's mine!" Arath said sharply, taking Hector's eye-stone from him and inspecting it. "Where did you get it?"

"I found it," Hector answered. "In the ground over there. Ettore said it's a good-luck charm, but it isn't Etruscan."

"It is," Arath said. "I mean, it's good luck, and it's Etruscan. All the Rashna children carry one, along with their first baby tooth and other special things, until they become adults. These are their protectors. They take care of you until you're grown enough to take care of yourself. Then at the manhood and womanhood ceremonies you give them up to the gods, and they get destroyed to show that you don't need your childhood protection anymore. I'm having my ceremony in two years," he added, "and then I won't need them. But until then, they keep me safe."

"Well," Hector said thoughtfully, taking his own stone from Arath's palm, "well, then, I guess this explains the 'why me' part of my question."

"What do you mean?"

"Don't you see?" Hector asked. "The eye is supposed to protect you. You lost it—I mean, you're going to lose it—you know what I mean."

Arath nodded.

"And then I found it—or I mean, I'm *going* to find it—" This was hopelessly confusing. "Anyway, I found it in my time. It made me find it. I bet it was looking for someone to protect you, since it couldn't do it by itself."

"But how did you get it?" Arath asked.

"I found it in the dig," Hector said. "I—"

At that moment he heard a voice from down in the village. It was a woman, and she was calling Arath's name.

"My *ati*—my mother," he said and scrambled to his feet, hastily dropping his lucky pieces back in the pouch. Hector stood up and shoved his own stone eye into his pocket.

"Where should I go?" Hector asked.

"Wherever you want," Arath answered. "With me, if you like. Remember, no one can see you when you're not in your own time. Just don't expect me to talk to you. They'd think I was talking to a *hinthial*." And he ran down the slope. Hector took off after him, feeling strange and almost weightless as he bounded down the hill. When he caught up with Arath, he saw him going into the door of the house next to the temple. The door swung shut behind Arath, and automatically Hector reached for the rope handle, but his hand went through it after a tiny hesitation.

Now what?

Well, if the man in the square could walk through him, maybe he could walk through the door. But that was just dream, wasn't it? And this time he was really here, really back in Etruscan time. Or was he? He was getting confused about what was a dream and what was reality— if time travel could be called reality.

Still, it was worth a try. He didn't want to be stuck here in the dusty street. He laid his hands flat on the door and pushed. It felt lighter than wood should feel. He pushed harder, and suddenly he popped through it to the other side.

Wow. It felt like going through a wall of Jell-O. Solid, but not really. It gave Hector a sick feeling, and he stood still for a minute to let everything settle. The room was dim, but enough light came through the small windows that his eyes soon adjusted.

Several mats were scattered on the dirt floor, and a stool stood by the fire. The walls were white but also stained with dark streaks from the smoke of the cooking fire, he supposed. There was very little decoration, just a kind of alcove by the door where a couple of figures like dolls were standing. He went closer and peered at them. The two crude wooden figures stared back blankly. Worn paint faintly indicated their eyes, mouths, and clothing. *A strange kind of thing to have in your wall*, he thought.

A small woman who had a dark braid down her back and was wearing a loose brown robe came in through another door on the opposite wall. Hector froze, but she gave no sign of seeing him. She spoke to Arath and then stooped over the fire, ladling something into a wooden bowl. From her tone, it appeared that she was scolding him. She didn't really sound angry, though. She handed the bowl and a spoon to Arath, who was squatting on a small rug, and passed her hand over his black hair. He looked up and smiled at her as he began eating what must be his breakfast.

Two other women, older than the first, appeared. They wore long robes with stripes down the sides, and one looked cranky. She held her hand to her cheek as the first woman soaked a piece of cloth in hot water that was steaming over the fire. She held it against the older woman's face, speaking soothingly.

Hector stood awkwardly in the middle of the room. Arath either couldn't see him anymore or was pretending not to, and the women gave no sign that they were aware there was a fifth person in the room. Hector cleared his throat. Arath's eyebrows shot up and Hector saw a little smile on his lips.

"So I can say anything I want," Hector said. Arath, still eating, gave an almost imperceptible nod.

"I can go wherever I want," Hector said. Arath nodded again.

"And no one can see me or hear me or anything." This time a little shake of the head.

"What's the matter with that woman?"

Arath opened his mouth as though yawning and pointed a finger at one of his back teeth.

"Toothache?" Hector guessed. Again a little nod and a smile.

At that moment Arath's mother straightened.

It was the same woman who had been wailing in the square in that terrible dream, and she was staring him right in the face.

12

Hector yelped and stumbled backward. But Arath's mother must have just happened to be looking in his direction, because she paid no attention to him.

Arath let out a snort of laughter. His mother said something that must have meant "What's so funny?"

Arath bowed his head over his bowl and scraped out the last of whatever he was eating. His mother took the empty bowl and said something else as she passed food to the other women. The one with the toothache groaned as she opened her mouth a tiny bit.

Arath nodded to his mother and went back out the door. Hector didn't want to repeat the creepy experience of pushing through wood, so he slipped out behind the other boy before it had a chance to close.

In those few minutes the town had come alive. It looked more like what Hector had seen on his first visit. Several women were carrying jugs on their heads. Four little children, naked except for strings of beads around their waists and leather pouches like Arath's dangling from their necks, followed, laughing and playing as they went. Two men were working on the wall again, and Hector could see that some time had passed since he had last been there, because they had almost finished the repairs.

"Where are we going?" Hector asked, but Arath just frowned and kept walking. Oh, right. He couldn't answer in front of all those people.

After only a few steps, Arath turned and ducked into the temple, Hector close at his heels. Its cool darkness was pleasant after those few minutes in the glaring sun. "Can you talk now?" Hector asked. As an answer, Arath made a slight motion with his hand.

Two large shapes were in front of them. Hector peered more closely and realized that he was looking at two men, both standing with their backs to him, hands raised to the ceiling, long black hair falling down their backs. On one, a gold armband glinted. The other man was shorter and more muscular. Neither paid any attention to the boys—or rather, to Arath, since they couldn't be expected to notice Hector.

They started talking rapidly and rhythmically, first one, and then the other. *They must be praying*, Hector realized. As his eyes grew accustomed to the darkness, he saw that the walls were painted with pictures of people. He walked hesitantly to one of the pictures, feeling that he probably shouldn't touch it and feeling uncertain about being there, even though no one but Arath could see him.

The painting showed some kind of party. In the middle a man was dancing, arms and legs thrown out at odd angles, feet flexed and long hands bent way back. Another man blew on a flute, and a woman was holding something that looked like a rattle.

Men and women were lying on couches, tables covered with food all around them. One woman's hand was stretched out in front of her toward a smiling man, and in her long, elegant fingers she delicately held an egg. Little naked children with flowers in their hair held jugs that looked just like the ones the women had been carrying outside. Something dark was flowing out of one of them. The colors were so bright that even in the semidarkness they were easy to see. Everything in them seemed to be moving and swirling, so that it was hard to believe that they were paintings and not living people.

Arath stood in silence behind the two men, as though waiting. After a few minutes, the shorter man lowered his hands and spoke to Arath in a normal tone, no longer the singsong of a prayer. Hector had no trouble catching the man's meaning. It was as though the longer he stayed in the past, the more he understood. He could tell that the man was asking Arath why he was late. Arath mumbled something like "I'm sorry." The other man turned around and glared at him, and even in the dim light, what Hector saw made his heart stop for a second and then start thumping rapidly.

This was the man who had dragged Arath away and

had been with him when those sickening screams came from the temple. Looking at his cruel face, Hector had no doubt that he was the one who had been beating the boy.

The man turned away, raised his hands, and started chanting again. It went on and on.

Hector took a hesitant step forward. Arath rolled his eyes, evidently exasperated at Hector's timidity.

Hector gathered together all his courage and said, "It's easy for *you*. You're used to people not seeing you." He flinched at the sound of his voice, but the men obviously didn't hear him, although Arath rolled his eyes again.

It was weird. He could go anyplace, do anything, and no one would ever know. He took another step. Still no reaction from the men. So he walked firmly forward and looked at the objects on the table in front of the men. Three small statues, only a few inches tall, stood stiffly in a row. They glittered so richly that Hector knew that they had to be made of gold. The figures were human, one male and two female, but unnaturally long and thin. The man and one of the women wore strange helmets with wing-like things sticking out on both sides and the top. The woman clutched a spear, and the man held a crooked stick. The other woman wore a long skirt and no top. All of their bodies were strangely flat, and their clothes were covered with tiny gold balls in beautiful patterns. Despite their size, the details were perfect.

Hector knew who they were from the book on the Etruscans that his mother had made him read. And even if he hadn't read the book, he would have recognized them. The man was Tinia, the sky god, Uni was the earth goddess, and Menrva was their daughter, a wise warrior and leader. And their statues were the most beautiful things Hector had ever seen. He reached out a hand to touch them, forgetting that he wouldn't be able to feel them. Arath cleared his throat sharply and Hector dropped his hand.

The cruel-looking man turned when Arath cleared his throat. Arath looked at him innocently. The man glared at him and then grunted something at the other man, who must be the priest, Arath's father. The priest said something that sounded like he was telling the man to forget it and handed Arath a small bowl with a kind of bump in the middle. Arath took it carefully, holding the edge with his thumb, and putting his middle and ring fingers into the depression on the back, as if he were holding a CD.

Hector's eyes were used to the dim light by now, and he saw that the wooden box the large man picked up next was beautifully carved and had gold on its corners. The man said some words quickly, in that singsong, and Arath and the other man repeated his words in unison. The priest opened the box and Arath scooped something out of it with the bowl. Hector stood on tiptoe to see over his shoulder. It was some kind of seeds or grain.

The priest closed the box and placed it carefully on the low table behind him. Next, he picked up a bright white cloth from the table and draped it over his head, hiding his face from view from the sides. Then the three of them turned and walked slowly to the door. First Arath's father went out, then Arath, then the taller man. Hector broke into a trot and slid out just before the door closed.

As Hector stumbled onto the portico, Arath flinched away from him and spilled some grain. The man cried out angrily and the priest spun around. When he saw what had happened, he barked something at Arath. The boy stood with his head bowed, looking like he was going to cry as the two men scolded him. The cruel-looking man lifted his arm threateningly, but the other one said something and he lowered his arm again, although he stood with his hands on his hips, scowling.

What's the big deal? Hector wondered. They could easily pick up the few grains that had fallen, and it looked like there was plenty more in that box, anyway.

The man grabbed the dish away from Arath and roughly spun him around by the shoulder so that the boy was facing the temple. He shoved Arath back into the building so hard that the boy tripped over the stone step and fell heavily to his knees.

"Hey!" protested Hector, forgetting that only Arath could hear him.

"Shut up," Arath said, and then clapped his hand over his mouth.

The man shouted something to the priest, pointing at Arath accusingly. Hector caught the word *hinthial* a few times, and another word, *aisna* or *eisna* or something, over and over again. Arath's father caught the man's arm and spoke sharply to him. He turned to Arath and said something that must have meant that he had to leave, for Arath ran out the door.

He raced back the way they had come, his head down, Hector hurrying after him.

"Hey, Arath," he said. At least *he* could still talk, even if Arath couldn't answer in public. "That guy is a real jerk—I mean, yelling at you just because you spilled a little of that stuff—"

Arath slowed to a fast walk and shot Hector a glare from beneath his dark brows that said "shut up" even more clearly than his earlier words. Hector stopped talking and followed him into the house. It was empty. Arath flung himself down on a mat and stared into the cold fireplace.

Hector waited until he couldn't stand it anymore. "So you want to tell me what that was all about?" he asked.

"I spoiled the sacrifice," Arath said, his voice jerking with the strain of not crying. "For my father, that is a terrible thing. His religion is the most important thing to him—more important than me, more important than my mother, more important than his own life. Then Cai heard what I said to you and told my father I was talking to evil spirits in their own language."

"That was Cai? The one who wants to be priest instead of you?" Arath nodded miserably.

"Why was that a mess-up?" Hector asked. "All you did was spill a little of that stuff."

"That *stuff* is holy grain," Arath said. "Didn't you see how I had to scoop it out?" Hector nodded. "Once it's been blessed it belongs to the gods and no one can touch it ever again. The bowl is specially made so you can scoop it without your fingers getting in it. And then to spill it on the ground—" He shook his head. "Well, it shows disrespect for the gods. And Cai said it means I'm not a worthy successor to my father. He hates me."

"You shouldn't be the priest just because you spilled some grain?" Hector couldn't believe it.

"There are other things too," Arath said, sitting up and wrapping his arms around his knees. "I can read even though no one ever taught me, and sometimes I'm in one place and just an instant later I'm in another place because I traveled in time in the meanwhile. And sometimes in my sleep I talk in other languages that I learned when I was time traveling, and people say I'm speaking with *hinthials*."

"With what?"

"*Hinthials*. What you would call ghosts or spirits or angels."

"Can't you just tell them about time travel?"

Arath shook his head, looking wretched. "Then they'd know I read the holy books," he said. "And I'm not the priest, so that's sacrilege."

His voice was getting fainter and fainter. Suddenly Hector was tired—more than tired. He felt like when he was a little kid after a day at the beach. He never realized how exhausted he was until he got in the car and found he couldn't hold his head up.

"Arath—" he said, but his voice was blurry. Arath looked at him sharply.

"Don't fight it," he said. "You won't win." It sounded like he was speaking from far, far away.

"Fight what?" Hector asked.

"Your own time is pulling you back," Arath answered.

"What?" Hector tried to say, but he felt himself being tugged harder, and then he was tumbling upside down, backward, every way—and then he was lying on the grass, and it was night. He could tell by the way the grass felt sharp on his skin and how sounds weren't muffled, and even by the clean, dry smell of the dirt under his face, that he was back in the twenty-first century.

13

Hector sat up, dizzy and muddleheaded. The sky was pale blue and birds were making a racket, so morning must be near. He'd better get back to Susanna's house and into bed before anyone noticed he was gone. Then he could think about everything that had happened and try to straighten it all out.

His footsteps were painfully loud, even on the dirt. He must have gotten so used to the dullness of sounds in Etruscan time that a real noise was almost deafening by contrast.

By the time he reached the house his calves were sore from the climb up the steep streets. He headed for the stairs, aching for bed.

"Heck?"

Oh, no. Just when he thought he was safe. He hesitated, his hand on the banister, then turned and went into the kitchen. His mother sat there, dressed, holding a cup of coffee.

"Where have you been?" she asked, an edge to her voice. "I woke up an hour ago and saw your door open. You weren't there. I've been going out of my mind with worry. Where have you been?"

He gestured vaguely behind him toward the town, the hill, the dig.

"Outside? At this hour? What were you doing out there?"

What would be the point of telling her? She would never believe him. She'd think he was crazy or was making up some story so he wouldn't get in trouble for wandering around in the dark.

But she was glaring at him. So he sat down at the table and told her about seeing Arath on top of the arch that day. Told her about Cai, the temple, and Arath's mother and his father, the priest. That he knew that Cai was going to hurt Arath terribly unless someone did something, that he, Hector, seemed to be the only one who could help, and that he appeared to have been chosen by Arath's protective eye-stone.

His mother kept her eyes fixed on him and once or twice acted as if she was going to say something. But she sat with her lips pressed tight until he finished.

"And then time pulled me back and dumped me in the field," Hector finished.

Silence. Finally she said, "Heck, now tell me what you've really been up to."

"But Mom," Hector protested, "I *did* tell you what I've been up to. It's true. I swear. I met an Etruscan boy named Arath . . . " His voice trailed off.

She stood up. "Honey," she said, in a patient tone, "lots of people have nightmares and even walk in their sleep, but it's not—they usually don't believe that their dreams are real. If you truly believe that this happened, that means you're—that something is going on with you and we're going to need to find someone to make you better."

"Better? What do you mean, 'better'?" Hector asked, his voice rising. "I'm not crazy! I never should have told you!"

"Oh Hector, cut it out," she said, turning to put her coffee cup in the sink. She stood with her back to him. "Lots of people need help with this kind of thing, and there's nothing to be ashamed of about seeing a psychiatrist or—"

"I don't need help," he interrupted. "I thought Arath was crazy at first but it turns out he's not, he's really an Etruscan. And you think I'm crazy but I'm not. I really went back to his time."

"Prove it, then," his mother said.

"Prove it? How can I?"

"Show me something you found there."

"I can't bring you anything," Hector said. "I'm there but not there. I can feel things, kind of—but I can't pick them up."

"Enough," his mother said. "That makes no sense. Think about what I said. Decide how important this fantasy is to you. If you keep telling me this time-travel stuff we'll have to find someone who can help you."

"What makes you think it's impossible?"

She threw up her hands in exasperation. "It just is, Hector. Time isn't a physical thing that you can walk around in."

Great, Hector thought. *Parents always say they want you to tell them things, but when you do they don't believe you. So I'll just stop talking.*

His mother was still glaring at him. "Oh, all right," he mumbled, looking down.

"Good," she said. "Now go upstairs and get cleaned up. Then come back down and have breakfast. We want to get to the dig good and early to get some work in before it gets too hot. You coming today?"

He nodded.

"Excellent," his mother said. "You'd better take advantage of it while you can. The foundation says that they've already spent too much money here, and they're threatening to close the dig in a week or two."

Hector rose and walked slowly to the stairs. As he put one foot on the bottom step, he turned around to try one last time.

"Mom," he said. "I do have an Etruscan thing." She raised a glowering face, but he went on. "It's this," and he pulled the stone eye out of his pocket.

She made an exasperated noise. "Oh, Hector," she said. "Now you're being just plain ridiculous. You didn't bring that back from some other time. You found it right here. And anyway, Ettore said it wasn't Etruscan. Nobody has ever found anything like it before."

"That's because they get destroyed when a kid has his manhood ceremony," Hector said.

"*What?*" his mother said. "That's nonsense. There's no evidence of a manhood ceremony among the Etruscans."

"There's no evidence of a lot of things among the Etruscans," Hector retorted. "You keep telling me that nobody knows much about them. So maybe—"

"I don't have time for this," his mother said. "I've got to get down to the dig. Have something to eat and then either come down there if you want or hang out here. Just don't give me any more silliness about traveling in time."

Fine, he thought as he sat on his bed and took off his shoes to pull on some socks. He flopped down on his back and stared at the ceiling. *No one ever listens to me anyway, so I should have expected this. I won't tell anyone else about Arath and Cai and traveling in time.* But a thought nagged at the back of his mind. He tried to push it away, but it returned.

What if she was right? What if he had just imagined Arath and all the rest?

No, that couldn't be. It was so real. He could still see the young men talking and wrestling, the women with jugs on their heads, Arath's mother smiling as she gave her son his breakfast. But if he were crazy, all those things would seem real to him anyway, wouldn't they?

He rolled over onto his belly. The stone eye dug into

his hip through his pocket and he pulled it out. He rolled it in his hands and stared into it thoughtfully. If you were crazy, how could you tell what was real and what wasn't?

Voices were coming from downstairs. It was his mother and Susanna, and he heard his name. He put the eye down on his bedside table, walked silently in his bare feet to the top of the stairs, and leaned over to listen.

"Don't worry, *cara*," Susanna was saying. "He is almost an adolescent. He is having difficulty finding out who he is, like all adolescents. This Etruscan boy must be a kind of fantasy hero to him. Soon 'Ector will be an adult and he will be too serious and he won't have these dreams anymore. And then I think you will miss your little boy with the good imagination."

"But Susi," his mother said, "he is so convinced that this boy is real and that he went back in time to an Etruscan village. Don't you think that's strange?"

"He needs attention," Susanna said. "Attention from you. You are always busy with your work, no? And you said that you were passing much time with Ariadne because she gave you problems. And maybe you were not with 'Ector so much then, no? He feels like no one listens to him. Perhaps that's why he thinks of a place where no one can see him or hear him, eh?" No answer. "What do you think, Betsy?"

"Well," his mother said slowly, "you could be right. Maybe I should be paying more attention to him. It's just that he's never given us any trouble."

"You should give him a prize for that—"

"A reward," Hector's mom said, but Hector could tell that she was correcting automatically and was really listening to Susanna.

"A prize, reward, what you like," Susanna went on, "for being good, instead of waiting for him to be bad before you pay attention."

So instead of going to the dig after breakfast, Hector found himself in Susanna's tiny car zooming first down narrow, winding roads and then on a modern highway. Fields whizzed by the small window, their light brown and green punctuated by flowers as bright red as jelly beans. Beyond the fields the blue mountains kept pace with the car. Hector glanced at the speedometer. The needle was on 110. "Mom, you're speeding!" he said.

She glanced down. "No, we're okay."

"A hundred and ten?" he asked, disbelieving.

"Kilometers, kiddo," she said. "That's about sixty-five. Perfectly legal. It just feels fast because the car is so small."

He settled back in his seat. If Arath had been a dream, as his mother thought, surely they would be too busy today for Hector to imagine seeing him. And Arath seemed to hang around the place where his village used to be. Maybe he couldn't leave it. Besides, Arath didn't know where Hector had gone. So either way, whether Hector was crazy or Arath was real, Hector was free of him for the day.

Somehow, he didn't find that thought comforting. He shifted in his seat and looked out the window, trying to get interested in the landmarks his mother was pointing out, but all he could think about was how real it had all felt.

No, he decided. He wasn't crazy. He just knew it. He knew he'd gone back in time and that Arath was a real boy—a real Etruscan boy. Hector squirmed. Well, it was out of his hands for today. He had to just push it out of his mind.

He hadn't thought he'd have a good time, but the trip turned out to be more fun than he had imagined. Florence was tan and brown and yellow, with lots of people speaking different languages. He and his mother went to a huge museum with painting after painting of beautiful blond women holding ugly babies, and then they sat at a metal table in a square filled with white statues streaked gray with pigeon droppings. His mother drank a coffee, and he had another orange soda. They bought a soft leather purse for Ariadne and a wild silk tie for his father, and for Hector a T-shirt with a picture of the head of the statue of David.

As they tried to find all the places his mother wanted to visit, they talked about Florence and the mobs of tourists, about how rotten jet lag felt, and about what everyone at home must be doing. About everything, that is, except Etruscans in general and time travel in particular.

So many people packed one narrow bridge lined with jewelry stores that Hector and his mother got stuck behind two women who had to be American, both of them clutching stuffed shopping bags. They looked exhausted as they teetered on their high heels on the uneven pavement. As Hector worked his way around one side of them and his mother around the other, the one near him said to the other, "Well, it was combat shopping, but it was worth it." He heard his mother snort with amusement.

There was one more museum to see, his mother had said. He protested until she told him that it had some Etruscan artifacts.

"All right," he said. "But can this be the last one?"

"Tired of combat museum-ing?" she said, and laughed as he groaned.

But this museum turned out to be worth it. Glass cases lined the walls, full of black pottery with fine lines making designs on the sides. They were such nice fat little things—cups and pitchers and plates—that he itched to pick them up, and he saw from the fingerprints on the glass that he wasn't the only one who had been tempted. *Bucchero*, his mother called it, and he silently mouthed the word after her. BOO-keh-roh. Poor man's bronze, she said it was.

But the jewelry was the most amazing thing. The brooches and bracelets were covered with tiny balls of gold, some making designs along lions' backs, others delineating facial features. A magnifying glass was tethered to one of the cases with fishing line and through it Hector could see that each ball was an almost-perfect sphere, just a little flattened where it joined the main piece.

His mother came up behind him. "Unbelievable, isn't it?" she said. He nodded, moving the magnifying glass slowly down the back of one of the lions.

"How could they do it so perfectly?" he asked.

"Come over here," she said.

He joined her at the next case. Hoping for more gold, he was disappointed to see two yellowish, curved objects with no decoration. One had a crack running down the middle of it. His mother said, "Look, that's how they did it."

"How?" he asked.

"See that long, curved piece?" He nodded. "It's made out of bone. They would put a tiny drop of gold at the top of the crack and let it run down, aiming it straight at the spot where they wanted the ball to land. As it rolled, it would cool off enough to stay round but would still be liquid, so it would attach itself to the jewelry."

"So how come it didn't splat when it landed?"

"See that other thing?" It looked like a small trumpet. "Another person would sit with that blower in his mouth, and the instant the gold hit the jewelry, he would puff out a little bit of air to cool it while it was still a sphere. Imagine—if he puffed too hard, he would blow it off and they'd have to start over again. And even a little drop of gold was valuable. But if he didn't blow hard enough, or blew too late, it would splat, as you said."

Unbelievable. His mother moved on as he stared, imagining how long it must have taken to make something with thousands of those little balls on it. He stayed there until the guard, a bored-looking man in a blue uniform, jangled a bunch of keys from the doorway and they had to leave.

It was dark when they got back in the car. Hector was tired from all the walking and stair-climbing. His mother must have been worn out, too, because they hardly talked for the whole long ride.

Hector tensed as they passed under the archway into Sporfieri, expecting to see Arath staring at him. But there was nothing, and nobody, out on the streets. And when he went to bed, his dreams were the normal kind of crazy thing that people usually dream, with no Etruscan boys and no human sacrifices and no temples with boxes of holy grain.

14

Hector lowered himself into the trench, clutching his tools. Ettore grinned up at him from where he was squatting in the dirt.

"Ready to be an archaeologist again?" he asked.

"Ready," Hector said, and grinned back.

"Did you like Florence?"

"It was cool," Hector said. "Crowded, though."

"That's the problem with having beautiful things," Ettore said. "Everyone wants to see them. But we're used to sharing our city. You should come back in the winter when it's mostly *fiorentini* there."

"Do you dig in the winter?"

"No," Ettore said. "But I think we won't dig here in the summer anymore, too."

"I know," Hector said. "My mom told me about the dig maybe closing."

Ettore nodded, a frown-line creasing the space between his eyebrows. "They say that my temple probably isn't a temple, just a house, and the garbage pile isn't interesting, even with the bones. They don't understand that the things we find there are the most useful. They want something exciting, like some jewelry. Even that painted wall wasn't enough for them. A picture of a priest that is so damaged you can't see what he is sacrificing. But so far, nothing. And we're running out of time." He shrugged, and then his forehead smoothed. "Let's not talk about sad things. Let's enjoy the time we have left. Okay?"

"Okay," Hector agreed.

They worked in companionable silence, broken only when Hector held something out to Ettore for examination. They found a few tiny pieces of pottery, but nothing out of the ordinary.

During a break, they sat on folding chairs under a tree. Hector pushed his sweaty bangs off his forehead. His skin felt sticky and his back ached. But it was a pleasurable ache, and the cold water tasted wonderful. After a while, Ettore asked Hector if he was still missing his friends back home.

"Some, I guess," he answered. "But I don't think they're doing anything as cool as archaeology this summer."

"So are you glad you came to Sporfieri?"

"I guess so," Hector said, then realized he didn't sound very enthusiastic. "I mean, it's nice here and all. I just wish that someone had listened to me when I said that I would rather stay home."

"Does it feel like no one listens to you?"

"It doesn't just *feel* like it," Hector said. "They don't."

"Just because people don't do what you want doesn't mean that they don't listen." Ettore tossed his empty water bottle into the recycling bin. "Sometimes they don't believe you or have some other reason not to do what you ask."

"It's frustrating, though," Hector said. "It's like being invisible when you try to say something and no one pays attention."

"I agree," Ettore said. "It's a big insult. And sometimes you have to *make* people listen, like to tell if someone is hurting you. If one adult won't hear you, you have to find another one who will. But usually, you must decide if what you are saying is really important. If it is, then keep telling people until someone listens to you. If not, let it get lost."

After lunch, Hector's mother said, "I could get used to this afternoon nap habit," as they climbed the hill to Susanna's house.

"I'm not sleepy," he said.

"Good time to get started on your summer reading, then." She laughed when he groaned.

His room was dark and cool. He opened the shutters to let in some light, careful not to leave enough of an opening for the summer sun to heat up the room. He opened his book. After a minute, he turned the page but then realized that he hadn't read a single word. He turned back and tried again.

No use. He couldn't concentrate. All he could think of was Arath and his own promise to help him. He hadn't seen Arath for a day and a half, or dreamed about him, either. What did this mean? He didn't like the only answer that occurred to him, but he forced himself to face it. What if, he asked himself reluctantly, what if Arath had come looking for him the day before and couldn't find him because he was in Florence? What if he couldn't come back now because in the meantime something had happened to him, and he had died before he could time-travel again?

Hector leaned out the window and looked down. Maybe Arath would be waiting below, like that other time. But no. The street was deserted. Hector tried to see over the roofs of the houses between himself and the dig, but all he could make out was the olive grove on the hill beyond it. He turned back to his book but gave up. He tossed it on the bedside table, where it banged into a pile of paper, socks, and something else. Something hard that bounced off the table, hit the stone floor with a *crack!* and then rumbled into a corner.

Hector went over and picked it up. Of course, it was the eye. He could have sworn that it glared at him accusingly. He stared into it.

"What?" he said. "What's the problem, eye?" There was no answer, but then he wasn't expecting one. He stared deeper into the black center, not blinking. The world swirled around him gently, as though he was just beginning to fall asleep. Things turned gray and soft and muted. Still he stared into the eye.

And then he was there. He was standing in a crowd of people, gathered together in a tight but silent group. Once again, the light was clear but strangely pale. A commotion arose from the edge of the square, and he looked over and saw Arath being dragged out of the temple, bedraggled, his lip cut and swelling, red marks starting to turn to bruises on his legs and arms. Blood seeped through his hair above one ear and trickled down his cheek.

Hector watched as Arath fell to his knees in the dirt. Red dust stained the boy's white shirt and his shoulders shook with silent sobs. In front of the watching crowd stood the tall, thin Cai, a sneer on his handsome face. Cai's black hair shone in the sunlight, and a gold bracelet glittered on his upper arm.

Hector's nostrils stung from the hot dust. Dread washed over him. How could he stop what was going to happen? The feeling of horror built up until he felt he would burst.

"No!" he shouted, but the others didn't seem to hear him. He ran into the crowd, tugging at arms, but no one paid any attention. So he gave up and he, too, fell silent and stared in the same direction as the rest of them, at Arath.

Hector could tell from the air of expectancy that everyone knew that something bad was going to happen.

Did they feel the same horror that he did? It was impossible to tell from their stony, expressionless faces. A woman fell to her knees, her hands raised to the sky, and she wailed in a thin, hopeless voice. The boy twisted in her direction and called out to her, "*Ati! Ati!*" She screamed, "*Arath!*" The other people drew away, looking at her from the corners of their eyes, if at all.

The temple door opened slowly, and the priest stepped out. He strode toward the boy kneeling in the dust. Arath raised his head, and his large dark eyes, shining with tears, shone in Hector's direction. Arath cried out as though surprised and struggled to raise himself to his feet. He failed. Hector took an involuntary step backward.

Arath's father was wearing a white cloth over his head and shoulders, and an animal skin that reached just below his knees. He was barefoot, and the reddish dust swirled around his feet. As he walked, he pulled a long knife from his belt. He stopped when he reached Arath, who was no longer calling out to Hector but was saying something in a pleading tone. The man paid no attention but instead grabbed the pouch that was hanging from the boy's neck and sliced through its strings. He hurled it hard to one side, and small objects flew out into the dust. They rolled and rolled with the force of the man's throw until they were out of sight.

When the man jerked to throw the pouch, the cloth hanging around his face fell back. Hector saw tears glittering in his dark eyes that were so like Arath's and saw that his mouth was pressed into a grim line. He had never seen an expression so bleak, a face that so clearly spoke of despair and sorrow and loss.

The man yanked the cloth forward again, hiding his tragedy from the crowd, and cried out, *"Flerchva ratum tur!"* He pressed one knee into Arath's back between his shoulders, then grabbed the long hair and pulled the boy's head toward himself, making his neck stretch like a bow. For one long second he hesitated, glancing at the wailing woman. Then his knife flashed downward.

15

Hector lurched with shock, and the eye rolled off his palm. He stared wildly around. For an instant he was confused to find himself in a small, white room, instead of in that bright, hot square.

"Oh, no!" he cried as the realization hit him. Somehow he'd been thrust brutally back to his own time. He scrabbled for the eye on the floor, desperate to go back to Arath, but when he turned it face up, it lay like a dead thing in his hand.

"Oh, *no!*" he cried again, feeling a stab in his heart. Why was the eye so lifeless? Did it mean that Arath had been killed and that it was too late to change anything now?

No. It couldn't be. The eye was supposed to protect Arath, and he, Hector, had been chosen as the means of that protection. He was not going to give up. He stared frantically into its center, picturing Arath, picturing the village, the people, Cai, Arath's father, his mother. *Come on, come ON,* he thought. *Take me there, take me back, let me do my job—*

He felt a tugging, and this time he welcomed it and

allowed it to pull him back into that timeless gray space as the world around him grew soft and translucent. Then everything solidified again. His heart thumped as vague shapes took form. Would he be in his room in Sporfieri, or in Arath's village?

He was sitting in the dust in the square. The sun was beating down hard, and heat shimmered from the road. No one was in sight. Was he too late? Had he arrived after Arath's father had killed his own son as harsh punishment for some crime and then had his body tossed into the garbage heap in disgrace?

No. Hector couldn't believe it. Even as his mind reeled at the horror of what he had seen—or had almost seen— he forced himself to think logically. The eye would not have brought him here unless he would still be able to help. That was what the eye was for—to protect Arath. It had failed once and was trying to make up for it. And Hector was the one who was going to have to do its work. The eye-stone must have brought him back to this time to fix whatever it was that had caused Arath's father to sacrifice him to the gods.

It had to be some kind of sacrilege. Arath had insisted that this was what mattered most to his father. It was hard to imagine that he would go so far as to knife his own son—Hector swallowed hard at the memory of that glittering blade—for anything less.

He stood and dropped the staring blue eye back in his pocket. He'd better keep a tight hold on it. What if he lost it? Would he be stuck here forever? The eye was supposed to protect Arath, not him. Would it return him to his own time if he failed? Arath had said he'd always be returned home, but he had seemed uncertain about some of the details of time travel. Was he wrong about this one?

Panic clenched him. *Well,* he told himself, trying to keep calm, *there's nothing I can do about that now. I'm here, and if I don't get swept back to my own time, I'll just find Arath and have him teach me how he got me to the present before. Or I can read it in those books.* He tried to silence the little voice that said, "What if you're too late and Arath's dead? Can you read Etruscan?"

He looked around the square, trying to quiet his fear. The longer he stood there, the calmer he felt. His pounding heart slowed, and the image of himself wandering alone through time dissolved. He had a job to do. No one could do it for him; no one could even give him advice.

But his confidence faltered as he realized that he had no idea what to do next. He took a step toward Arath's house, then stopped. He shuddered as he remembered the weird feeling of shoving through the closed door. He would wait until someone opened it and then go in with them.

He sat back down. Absentmindedly, he tried to trace a pattern in the dirt, but his fingers passed over the fine red dust without making a mark. He slapped his hand down as hard as he could, but when he lifted it, the ground was as smooth as before.

Where was everybody? Maybe they were like the modern Italians and slept in the heat of the day. It was uncomfortable in the blazing sun, even though he was pretty sure he wasn't feeling the heat as strongly as if he were completely there. The hour of Pan. Maybe people from cold northern countries had superstitions about midnight because of their long, dark nights, but it made sense for people from hot places to dislike the middle of the day instead.

Something moved down in the square. Hector froze before remembering that he didn't have to worry about being seen. He got to his feet and walked down the hill, cautiously approaching the temple. As he stepped into its shadow he nearly ran into a tall figure moving stealthily down the alley between the buildings. Hector gasped and flattened against the wall. But he needn't have worried; the man obviously didn't see him. It was Cai. Hector could tell by the silence of his progress and the way he was looking around that he was very anxious not to be noticed.

What could that jerk be up to? Hector drew a deep breath and followed. Cai opened the door of the temple just wide enough to squeeze in, then pulled it shut softly behind him. Hector hesitated. He thought of the sick feeling of forcing his body through the wood. *Cai's probably just doing some priest thing in there*, he told himself. *I'll wait till he comes out.*

The door opened again and Cai's head poked around it. The man warily looked left, then right, and then he slid out the door. He was clutching a cloth-wrapped bundle to his chest. He stepped lightly down the stairs and headed toward Arath's house. He stayed close to the walls and kept looking over his shoulder. But no one was out. The sun was still scorching, and the little breezes that swirled the dust around weren't enough to cool the air.

Cai held his ear against the door to Arath's house for a long minute. Then he gently pressed against it and went in, letting the door close. *Great*, Hector thought, but this time he knew he had to follow, so he went through the door itself.

He emerged into the darkness of Arath's house feeling as if someone had kicked him in the gut. Where was Cai? Hector could see something bulky on the floor near the fireplace. He leaned over to peer at it and drew back with a start when he realized that it was Arath's mother. She gave a little snore. *The Italian habit of taking an afternoon nap must go back a long, long way*, he thought. Then he heard a rustle behind him. He turned and saw another lump on the floor. Arath, he realized. But something hovered over the sleeping boy.

It was Cai. He was squatting and gently lifting one corner of Arath's sleeping-mat. Cai reached into the pouch with his free hand and drew out one of the gold statues that belonged on the table in the temple. He slid it carefully and silently under the mat, near the wall. He did the same with the other statues and then straightened. Silently he crossed the room and let himself out the door.

Hector felt hot with rage as he realized what Cai was doing. The next time people went into the temple, they would notice that the statues were gone, and Cai would find some way to make sure that Arath's house was searched. When they were found, everyone would think that Arath had stolen them. And if they made such a fuss over a little spilled grain—well, he could just imagine how they would react at the theft of their precious statues. He shuddered at the memory of that knife arcing toward Arath's throat.

It was good that Hector had seen the whole thing, or Cai's scheme would have worked. Now all Hector had to do was wake Arath up and tell him what had happened, and Arath could take the statues back to the temple before anyone knew they were missing. Finally Hector knew what he had to do.

"Arath!" he whispered. No good. The boy didn't stir. "Arath!" he said louder. Still nothing. He turned cold as he thought, *Did Cai kill him?* But then Arath turned over without waking. He must be a sound sleeper.

"Arath!" Hector called again. Nothing. Frustrated, he leaned over and shouted right in his ear, "Wake up! Cai is trying to get you in trouble!" He tried to grab Arath's shoulder and shake him, but his hand closed around nothing solid, nothing flesh and bone.

"This isn't funny," Hector said desperately. "Cai's framing you. I saw him. You've got to—" But he stopped. It was obvious that Arath wasn't ignoring him. He just plain couldn't hear him.

Hector had finally found out what he was supposed to be doing in Etruscan time, but he couldn't do it.

16

It made no sense. If he had been led into the past to save Arath, why couldn't he do what he was supposed to do?

Arath groaned and rolled over again. Maybe the next time he moved he would bump into the little statues and wake up. Then maybe he would discover them himself and return them to the temple. Well, if it were that easy, it would have happened like that without all the bother of Hector having to go back in time. No, there was still something that he was supposed to do. There *had* to be. He just couldn't figure out what.

Hector went to the dark corner and squatted by Arath's sleeping-mat, examining it more carefully. It was just an ordinary brown piece of cloth, not too clean, and rumpled in the middle where Arath was lying. He touched the corner that Cai had lifted. It felt lumpy, with the statues heaped up underneath. He tried lifting it, even though he knew his hand would go through it. Sure enough, his thumb and fingers squeezed together, passing right through the cloth.

Yuck. He shuddered and wiped his fingers on his shirt. It felt comfortingly solid compared with that mushy cloth on the floor. But—something hadn't felt mushy. He sat back on his heels and thought. Was it his imagination or had his fingers grazed something hard and cold as they passed through the cloth?

He didn't really want to do it again, but he had to try. He pressed down on the mat. For a moment the fabric resisted, but then, as though the fibers had shifted and parted, his hand went through.

And stopped on a hard little object.

It had to be one of the statues. What had the three gods said to him in the mist? "We are not of this time, and we are not of that time." So maybe he could touch them no matter where—or when—he found them. But that had been only a dream. There must be some other explanation.

And then it came to him. He pulled the eye out of his pocket. Arath could hold it and move it, even in Hector's time. Maybe this was because Hector had found Arath's lucky piece in the twenty-first century *and* it had existed in ancient days. So it was in both places at once, meaning that someone from either time could handle it. That would explain why he could kind of feel the dirt, but not really—a lot of it was probably the same dirt in his time as in Arath's. But not all of it. He could feel only the parts of it that were just as they had been more than two thousand years ago. That's why it didn't feel exactly solid.

But he could go through the door, because it had been destroyed long before he was born. There was no way that wood left out in the open could last for so many centuries. And the leaves and things—they were gone long ago too. It was just objects that existed in both times that he could feel when he was in the past.

Hector fought down the excitement that was swelling in his chest. Okay, now he knew why he could feel the statues. They must exist in both his time and in Etruscan time. So they were solid to him, even though he was modern and they were ancient. But how did this help? He could feel them, but that didn't mean that he could do anything with them. And in any case, they were stuck under the mat. He reached through the cloth again and felt his fingers wrap around the statues. He tried to pull them out.

No good. His hand was of another time and could pass through the mat, but the gold statue was solid and wouldn't come out, no matter how he tugged. An ancient piece of gold can't go through something else ancient, like cloth. Reluctantly, he let go of the statue he was grasping and heard the soft thud as it hit the ground. It wasn't loud enough to wake Arath, though.

Maybe he could pull one out along the floor. So he slid his hand along the ground, trying to work it under the cloth. He pushed hard, keeping his fingers firm against what he hoped was the dirt floor, moving them forward bit by bit toward the lump of statues. In a few seconds he was rewarded by the feel of something solid. He grasped the statue once again and pulled it along the floor, out from under the cloth, which rippled as the solid object moved under it. The gold figure slid out as easily as the stick from a melting ice-cream bar.

In his hand was one of the female deities, the one wearing the winged helmet. "Menrva," he breathed, and set the figurine carefully on the floor. Then he pulled out the other two. There they were, all three of them lined up. He squatted back and looked at them.

He couldn't believe his luck. Now he had something solid. He could poke Arath with them and wake him up, and then Arath would take them back to the temple. He picked up the three figurines, surprised at how heavy they were for their size.

But then Hector became aware of voices outside, people talking, some laughter. What if Arath woke up and sat in confusion before realizing that he had to take the statues back? What if someone came in and saw them in the meantime? Worst of all, what if his mother woke up and saw statues dancing around in Hector's invisible hands? No, there had to be something else he could do.

And he had to hurry. Was there somewhere in this little room to stash them? It was pretty bare, and any hiding place—a cooking pot or a pouch—would be instantly obvious to anyone coming in to search. The first thing to do, then, was to get them out of there and later return them to the temple himself, before Cai had a chance to accuse Arath of stealing these most holy objects. He dreaded the thought of going through the closed door, but there was nothing else to do, so he gritted his teeth and forced himself partway into it.

He stopped with a jolt as the statues knocked into the door, still on the inside of the hut. He gripped them more tightly and just managed to keep from dropping them. His hands holding the little gods were still inside the house. He shoved himself back into the dark hut and stared at them angrily.

"Damn!" he said, and instantly felt better. No one could hear him anyway, so he said it again. "Damn!" Now what?

Then he noticed that the back door, the one that Arath's mother had used the other day, was slightly ajar. The opening was too small for Hector, but it was plenty wide enough for the tiny figures. He set them down on the floor and pushed them, one by one, onto the outside step, praying that nobody was looking in that direction. Then he threw himself through the wood, in his haste hardly noticing the shivery feeling.

He was in a dark and dirty alley, and some people were there. No one was paying attention to him, or rather, to the three tiny statues on the step. Instead, they were hurrying toward the temple, where loud voices were shouting. They sounded terribly angry. Someone must have noticed that the statues were gone. That terrible Cai must have already told his lies about Arath stealing them. There was no way Hector could put them back now with everyone gathered around the temple like that. What should he do with them? Drop them in a well? But then he could never retrieve them. Maybe he should take them back to his own time for now, until he had a plan.

The first thing he had to do was get them away, and then he could figure something out. Pretty soon people would be coming to Arath's house. They would see the statues on the doorstep. He scooped them up and held them close to his belly, hunching over. He didn't know if that would give them his invisibility, but it was worth a try. And still bent over, he ran blindly away from the crowd, away from the noise and danger.

He slowed down and caught his breath as he looked around. Where was he? He searched for landmarks. Oh, good, there was the boulder. He could hide behind it with the figures, moving around it if anyone approached, and wait until nightfall before deciding what to do.

But suddenly he felt that strange tugging, as though an undertow in the ocean were dragging at him. He stared at his hands in horror as they became translucent. One by one the gold statues fell through his fingers, first Tinia, then Uni, and finally Menrva. They lay in full sight of anyone passing on the road.

"No!" he shouted. "I'm not ready yet!"

He made a huge effort to pull himself back. Everything was fading. He put his hand in his pocket, searching for the familiar, hard lump of the blue eye. As he wrapped his fingers around it, the weak feeling subsided slightly, and he saw with relief that his body was becoming more solid.

Although the tugging wasn't as strong as before, it was still there. He knew he didn't have much time. And he knew that he couldn't take the statues to the present with him. They would just fall from his hands as he drifted away. He had to hide them where no one from this time would find them until he could think what to do. Frantically, he looked around. People walked near this boulder frequently; he could tell by the dusty paths around it. If he just dropped the statues, someone would be sure to find them. Then all sorts of questions would come up, and that sneaky Cai would be sure to think of some way to make everyone believe it was Arath's fault.

Maybe Hector should leave the statues on top of the rock. He shoved them into his pocket. He tried to pull himself up the side, but it was too high and steep.

The dragging started up again, stronger than before. He fought the pull of time the way he'd fought the downward pull of his eyelids when he was first struggling with jet lag.

He looked up at the boulder. The rough gray rock was taller than it would be later, in his own time. Probably dirt was going to drift around it during all those decades between now and the twenty-first century, covering it partway up the sides. He circled the rock closely. Suddenly, his foot slipped into a little hole at its base.

Well, that would have to do until he could come up with a better plan. The pulling was getting worse, and he knew he couldn't resist it much longer. He carefully poked each statue into the hole, pressing them down into the soft earth as far as he could. A little red dirt fell around them, covering their glitter. He stood back and looked down. Was it enough to keep them out of sight until he could come back and find a way to return them to the temple?

Not a glint of gold shone through the red dirt, not a shadow—nothing. The voices from the town grew fainter, and the colors around him faded and then swirled around him. The next minute he was sitting on the floor of his room in Sporfieri, with his summer reading book lying open on the bedside table.

17

Hector leaped to his feet. He had to get back and find a better hiding place for the statues, or better yet, return them to the temple. Maybe he could go at night, when no one was around, and sneak them in with less risk. But most importantly, he had to see what happened to Arath. He held the eye, staring into it wildly.

Nothing. The eye looked like what it was, a lump of rock. He tried again. Still nothing.

He had failed. Arath would never come again. He had died a couple of thousand years ago, tortured and executed for something he hadn't done. That must be it, because something was keeping him from coming back to Sporfieri. Now that Arath was dead, the eye had nobody to protect and no reason to pull Hector back in time.

Cai must have told everyone that Arath had stolen the statues, and the people must have searched Arath's house. Even if the gods weren't found there, Cai could have said that Arath had hidden them someplace or destroyed them.

Hector stifled a sob in his pillow.

"'Ector?" It was Susanna.

He didn't want to see anyone but didn't know what else to do, so he said, "Come in."

She cracked the door and looked in. "We decided to rest for less time so we can perhaps find things before they close the dig the next week. Do you like to come?"

He nodded and got up. Better than lying there in that stuffy room, imagining what had happened to Arath.

"It's still hot," Susanna said. "You can wait until later, if you like."

"No," he answered. "I'll come now. Maybe I'll find another sherd and someone will give you more money."

"That would be good," she said. But she didn't sound convinced.

She was right about how hot it was. The heat slapped Hector's face as he jumped down into the trench.

"Wow," he said.

"Wow," agreed Ettore. "Why don't you wait until the sun has moved and we're in the shade?"

"But *you're* in here," Hector pointed out.

"I am accustomed," Ettore said. "You are not. Sit in the shade and have some water."

Hector didn't feel like arguing, so he sat under the tree near the cooler. He looked down toward the olive grove and wished that Arath would appear, even though in his heart he knew it would never happen again. Arath would have come before now if he could have. He must have died that day.

The sun was almost directly overhead, so the tree cast little shade and didn't provide much relief. The dry grass felt like crepe paper. The biggest patch of shade was by the boulder. Hector looked at it with loathing. Rotten rock. If only he'd found a better place to leave the statues.

Despite the heat and the stillness of the air, he suddenly felt the hairs on his arms stir with goose bumps.

He had left the statues under the boulder. What if they were still there? Gold didn't rot, did it? They *had* to still exist. If they weren't around in both Etruscan time and Hector's time, he wouldn't have been able to shove them into the dirt on that awful day.

He went back to the trench. "Ettore?"

"Mmm?"

"Is it okay if I dig over there?"

Ettore looked up over the edge of the trench. "Over where?" Hector gestured to the boulder. "Why there? There is no point. You never find things in that kind of place. Better to try where we have already found objects."

"But I think maybe I can find something there."

"What makes you think that?"

"I just think so, that's all," Hector said, knowing he was sounding like a kid.

Ettore said a little sharply, "Hector, if you really want to help, you must do what the person with experience says. There is no point in digging by that rock. Now either help one of the others who is working in the shade or go back to the house."

Hector almost gave up. But Ettore himself had said that when something was important, you had to keep trying, no matter what. And this was important.

Susanna, who had been talking to someone in another trench, came up.

"*Che caldo*, eh?" she said, and wiped a handkerchief across her glistening face. "Are you too hot to dig, 'Ector?"

"He wants to work near that big stone," Ettore said.

"Why there?" asked Susanna, like Ettore.

"I just feel like I'll find something," Hector said. The two adults looked at each other. He held his breath. *Please listen to me,* he begged inwardly.

"Well," Susanna said, "you found that sherd after I and Ettore didn't see it for two days. You have a good eye." *Please,* Hector thought. *Please let me dig there.* Susanna turned to Ettore. "I think we can permit it, don't you?"

Ettore made an exasperated face. "I don't see why you want that place," he said, "but Susi is the boss, and if she says it's okay, it's okay. Just stay in the shade so you don't get too hot."

Hector couldn't promise that, so he didn't say anything. He just collected a trowel and some extra water bottles. He carefully put the bottles in the shade, hoping to keep them from turning warm too fast. He walked around the rock. It was huge. How could he hope to find those three tiny statues?

Where exactly had he buried them? He looked back toward the dig. If that was the temple, and the road in Arath's time had come out this way—he measured the distance with his eyes—and then he had circled around the boulder, the hole must be on the other side. Great, the sunny side. Nothing to be done about that, though.

He wished he'd made a mark on the rock when he had buried them, but it was too late to think of that. Any mark he'd made most likely wouldn't have lasted all these centuries, anyway. Not like the spray-painted ANGELA TI ADORO, which would probably still be there when the world came to an end. He squatted down and started to dig.

The ground wasn't too hard here, fortunately. He scraped a wide area right near the boulder and stuck in the point of his trowel. He dug and dug until the heat made his head swim and little dots of light danced in front of his eyes. He went back to the shady side and drank half a bottle of water, then dumped the rest on his head.

"What on earth are you doing?" It was his mother, and she didn't sound happy.

"Ettore said I could."

"I don't care what Ettore said," she answered. "It's much too hot for this. You look awful. Go back to the house and rest."

"Please, Mom," he said, trying not to sound like a begging little kid. "Please. The dig is about to close and I'll never get to do this again. This is my last chance."

"But Heck—"

"Please," he pleaded. "Why don't you ever listen to me? This is something I really want to do. I'll be careful. I'm drinking lots of water and I just got my head all wet."

She hesitated. "Hector, honey," she said finally. "I do listen to you. Really. It's just that I don't want you to get sick."

"Just half an hour more," he said. "Then I'll stop. I promise."

"All *right*! I give up." She took off her broad-brimmed hat and plopped it on his head. "At least wear this to keep your brain from frying."

He knew he looked totally ridiculous, but the shade on the back of his neck did feel good.

"Thanks, Mom," he said, and meant it.

"Half an hour, Heck," she warned him.

But it turned out that he didn't need that much time. His mother had barely gotten out of sight when his trowel hit something hard.

He threw down the tool and dug and scratched with his hands. As the sides of the hole got deeper, the soft, red earth slid down as fast as he could dig it out. He dumped in some water and scooped out the resulting mud with shaking hands.

And then he saw a glint of gold. Unmistakably gold. Time seemed to stand still.

He didn't dare take his eyes off the sparkle. He was afraid it would disappear.

"Ettore!" he called. "Mom! Susanna!" He called louder. "I found something!"

He heard footsteps behind him. "What did you find?" Ettore asked in a tired voice. Hector pointed with a trembling finger. Ettore bent over and peered into the hole. "I don't see anything," he said. Hector's heart sank. Were the statues going to be invisible to everyone but him?

But just then Susanna came up and said, "What is that thing there that is—" she turned to Ettore. "How do you say *scintillando?*"

"Shining," he answered. "But I don't see anything shining."

Hector reached in and scooped out another lump of mud, revealing to even the most tired, sun-dazzled eyes a tiny gold arm holding a crooked stick.

Everything got confused after that. Ettore stood up and shouted something in Italian over his shoulder, and a woman came running with his tools. Ettore handed them to Susanna, who dug and prodded and scooped and at last gently, tenderly, pulled out the little male god.

"Tinia," breathed Hector. Susanna glanced at him sharply. The others pressed forward to see. No one seemed to mind that the heat of all their bodies made it practically impossible to breathe.

"*Oh, che bello,*" said one of the young women, and another voice said, "*Oui, c'est très, très beau,*" and then other voices chimed in, in various languages.

Susanna kept scraping and digging carefully and pulled out another statue. *Uni,* thought Hector. In another few minutes, Susanna was holding the small figure of Menrva. She handed it along with the other two to Ettore, who held them as though he was afraid they would break. She turned back to dig again.

"There aren't any more," Hector said, before he thought.

"How do you know?" Susanna asked.

"W-w-well . . ." stammered Hector.

"Well what?" Ettore said.

"Well, there were three important gods, weren't there? And you've found three statues."

"True," Susanna said. "But I still think we should assure ourselves, don't you?"

Hector nodded. It couldn't hurt, even though he knew there was no point. He got up and joined the crowd. Ettore was gently rubbing mud off the little gods and pointing out details to the others, who were nodding and looking and standing on tiptoe to see. They moved aside to let Hector in, as though he were a celebrity. One man slapped him lightly on the shoulder and said, "Bravo, molto bravo," and others joined in saying words in other languages that must mean the same thing.

"Do you think they're really Etruscan?" someone asked.

"Without a doubt," Ettore answered. "Look at the encrustation," and he indicated the tiny gold balls that made up the decoration. "And their faces and their clothes—they are certainly Etruscan, unless our friend

Hector has learned how to make beautiful forgeries." A few of them laughed, but happily and with no mockery.

"Hector." It was his mother. She took her hat off his head. He had forgotten he was wearing it. The evening breeze had sprung up, and it felt delicious against his damp hair.

"Why on earth did you think to dig there? Really."

He hesitated a moment. Should he try again?

"They were there all the time," was all he could manage.

She studied his face for a moment. Then she laughed.

"Maybe that eye you found is Etruscan after all and it helped you see Etruscan things. You think?" She gave his shoulder a playful shake. "You sure have great intuition. You've saved the dig. Do you know that? These are extraordinary, wonderful objects. No one has ever seen anything like them before. The foundation will be sure to fund more work now."

"Great," Hector said. He wanted to be more enthusiastic and really, he *was* glad for Ettore and Susanna and the rest, but he couldn't stop thinking about Arath. The Etruscans in Arath's village were already suspicious of him and the way he seemed to talk with *hinthials*. Cai's accusation of stealing the statues must have been the last straw.

They wouldn't believe him even if he swore he didn't touch those little gods, Hector thought, his stomach hardening with misery and with held-back tears. *Nobody ever listens.*

18

Hector couldn't shake his gloom, even when reporters and photographers showed up at the dig the next day. Someone had cleaned the mud off the statues, and he had to stand next to the table where they were displayed on a black cloth to have his picture taken with them. Over and over they asked him why he had chosen that particular place to dig, and over and over he said, "It just seemed like a good spot, that's all." Everyone seemed satisfied with this answer, weak though it sounded to him. But he knew there was no point in telling the truth. No one would listen to him, any more than they must have listened to Arath.

The next day, Susanna packed the little gods in sheets of bubble wrap and put them in a wooden box. Two silent men, wearing camouflage outfits and carrying guns, arrived in the afternoon and drove the statues away to Florence in an armored car. His father called and said that Hector had been on CNN.

With the statues gone, the excitement died down and the archaeologists got back to work. Their energy had returned with Hector's discovery, and new volunteers showed up to carve more trenches into the earth. Ettore managed a team of four of the more experienced people who were excavating the temple. Two different foundations and a university were offering to fund the dig.

Even though the danger of being closed down had passed, there was still a sense of urgency. A lot of the archaeologists were professors and graduate students who would have to leave soon to go back to their universities all over the world. Now that the "golden statue find" was making headlines, the archaeologists wanted to take advantage of every minute left to them to see if they could come up with something equally spectacular. One of the students rigged up an awning with cots under it at the edge of the dig. That way, they could take their breaks without going all the way back up to Sporfieri.

Hector started bringing his summer reading book down to the shady spot and after lunch, while the others dozed or chatted quietly, he tried to get interested in the story of some kid and his troubles with a gang. The situation was so far removed from the quiet heat of central Italy that it seemed like a dream, and he couldn't follow it.

It was their last day in Italy. Hector's mom was up at the house packing and had told him to get down to the dig and out of her way. It was the hot part of the day, so all the cots were taken by someone else, but he didn't mind stretching out on the cool earth. At least there were no chiggers in Italy. He'd be back in Tennessee soon and wouldn't be able to sit on the grass for months, until a frost killed all the invisible biting things. *Odd how something you can't even see is such a pain,* he thought.

He flopped over onto his belly and pulled the stone eye out of his pocket.

Well, at least he had something to remind him of Arath. *I did my best,* he tried to console himself. *I just ran out of time.* Arath would be dead now, anyway, whether Hector had succeeded or not. Dead for more than two thousand years.

Somehow, the thought didn't console him.

It was so hot. He couldn't concentrate on his book, and anyway the pages were getting droopy and sticky from the damp heat. He lay back and closed his eyes. The voices of the archaeologists in the nearby trenches became vague, the sounds mixing up and making no sense. The syllables sounded in a singsong rhythm, guttural consonants melting into liquid vowels. *It sounds like Etruscan,* he thought drowsily. And then he sat up, suddenly alert. It *was* Etruscan, not just mixed-up German and Italian and French and English.

In front of him, the small village had sprung up again. But the broken wall was now neatly mended and painted a cheerful orange. The laughing children and wrestling men were gone, but there was a crowd of people. Hector shrank back, dreading to see Arath tied up and helpless again.

But it was different this time. The crowd wasn't the silent, apprehensive group of that awful day. The people were dressed in what had to be their finest clothes, and gold glittered on their arms and earlobes and in their black hair. The littlest children wore shiny stone necklaces. Hector heard excited talk and laughter, but fuzzily, as though it were coming from a radio that wasn't quite tuned to the station.

As though at some invisible signal, everyone hushed and turned expectantly toward the temple. A tall figure stepped out of the shadowy interior and through the door as the crowd burst into high-pitched cheers. It was a shirtless man wearing a gray skirt that fell to his knees. He was tall and lean, with a smooth, hairless chest. *A teenager, or a bit older*, Hector thought. A dazzling white cloth draped over his head hid his face. A gold band shone on his upper arm, making Hector shrink back as he thought, *Cai?* But no, this man was much younger and more slender than the evil would-be priest.

In his right hand the man held a bowl. Even from that distance, Hector could see that it was filled with yellow grain. The man appeared not to notice the erupting crowd but stood quietly for a moment at the top of the stairs. Then he came down the short flight. The crowd fell silent again and moved aside to let him advance to the big stone fireplace in front of the temple.

Here the man stopped. He extended his arm and slowly poured the grain into the flame. Hector caught a faint whiff of something that smelled like burned popcorn. The man set the bowl down carefully and raised both his arms.

As he looked up at the sky, the cloth slid off his head, and Hector took an involuntary step forward. There was something about that man who was making the sacrifice. He looked—well, he looked like Arath. Older and more serious, but definitely Arath.

Arath looked solemnly around the crowd. When his gaze reached Hector he stopped and stared. Did he see Hector, or did he just happen to be looking in that direction? Hector couldn't tell, and now he felt himself waking up. He fought the growing feeling of coming back to consciousness as hard as he had fought the pull of time. But it was no use. As his dream faded, he saw his own hand reach out to Arath, the stone eye in his palm. He watched the eye slide off and bounce in the red dirt and roll slowly away as the world turned and turned around him until it became the middle of a hot day at the end of the summer, with his mother teasing him for falling asleep.

19

"Are you ever going to wake up?"

Hector rolled over and rubbed his eyes. He wished he could hold on to the dream and believe for just a little longer that Arath had survived to grow up and become a priest. But the feeling of relief slid away as the misery of knowing he had failed took over again.

"You're going to have to get out of this afternoon nap habit when we get home," his mother said. "After all, they don't have naps in school after kindergart—"

A shout from the dig interrupted her. "Susanna!" called Ettore's voice, hoarse with excitement. "Susanna! *Vieni qui! Ho trovato qualcosa!* Betsy! I found something! Come see!"

Hector, still groggy, turned to look as his mother took off at a trot toward Ettore. Susanna was already there, and they moved aside to let his mother see what Ettore was holding. Hector's fuzziness disappeared as he ran to join them.

Ettore was squeezing water over an object about the size and shape of a notebook. As the dirt washed away in reddish streaks, Hector saw that it was a piece of metal.

"Let me see," Hector's mother said, and Ettore handed her the metal plate. She caught her breath.

"What is it?" Hector asked.

"Bronze," Susanna said. "There's written something on it, see?"

"What does it say?" Hector said. His mother was peering at it, her lips moving slightly.

"I can't make out all the words," she said. "The patina is pretty thick. But some of it's legible. Let's see—it says something about *aisar*—that's 'gods,' and *turn celu Arath cvil*— that means this was dedicated by a priest named Arath—"

"What?" Hector interrupted. "Named what?"

"Arath," said his mother. She leaned over the tablet again and then stopped and looked at Hector. "Wasn't that the name—" She stopped again. "Didn't you—?"

"Come *on*, Betsy," Ettore broke in. "What else does it say?"

Hector's mother was still looking at him.

"Betsy!" Susanna sounded even more impatient than Ettore. "*Su, andiamo!*"

His mother turned back to the tablet. "And then something about that same priest, Arath, taking a journey—no, it seems to be *not* taking a journey, about the gods preventing him. Then some words: *alpnu, ruva, thuleri*—" She broke off and read a little more, frowning. "It's hard to say exactly what it means without studying it more closely. Something about thanking a brother from a foreign land and about a demon or evil spirit being chased away or fleeing or something. It's a demon I've never heard of before, with a name like Kai. You ever hear of a demon called Kai?" Ettore shook his head.

Susanna shrugged. "So what does it mean?" she asked.

"I'll have to examine it some more," Hector's mother said. "First let me copy down what I can make out."

"I'll help," Hector offered. They settled under the awning, and he sat on a cot, holding the bronze plate upright on his lap.

"Oh, and look what also I found." Ettore had come up behind him. He handed Hector his stone eye. Hector turned it over, feeling the now-familiar weight. His hand shook. He didn't understand. How had Ettore gotten it? Had he taken it from him while he lay under the shelter, dreaming or time traveling, or whatever it was he was doing?

"It *is* yours, isn't it?" Ettore asked, watching him closely. "I recognized the crack."

Hector nodded. "Where did you find it?" he asked.

"In the trench in front of the temple," Ettore answered. "But it was inside the dirt, not on top." Hector rolled the blue-and-white ball in his hand, still not understanding. He had lost the eye under the awning, far away from the temple area. It couldn't have rolled all the way down to the trench, could it?

Unless—the thought came to him so suddenly he felt dizzy—unless he had really lost it more than two thousand years ago, not today, and in front of the temple, not under the awning. In his mind, he watched it roll away again, toward that grown-up Arath. Had it gotten trampled and lost in that eager crowd? Had Hector even found it that first day he was digging? Or was it waiting here for Ettore to find it today? And if Hector didn't find it, how could he lose it for Ettore to find it again?

He thought he heard a soft voice say, "Time doesn't work like that," followed by equally soft laughter, but when he whipped his head around, he saw nothing. He suppressed a smile. *You don't know everything about time, Arath*, he thought as Ettore squatted next to Hector's mother and helped her decipher the letters.

Hector had to fight to keep from grinning as he turned the tablet where his mother indicated to give her the best view. He understood what it said, and his mother was basically right, even if she misunderstood some things. Arath *had* wanted to come see him again, but for some reason he hadn't been able to make the journey. Maybe the stone eye knew that Arath would be all right and didn't need Hector to travel in time again. He didn't suppose he'd ever know for sure. But it didn't matter.

"Mom?" Hector asked a little later, after Ettore had gone to talk to some of the archaeologists.

"Hmm?" she said.

"Do you really think the name of this town means 'city of sacrifice'?"

"What are you talking about?" She put down her pencil and gave him her full attention for once.

"You know, when we first came here and Susanna asked you what you thought 'Sporfieri' meant and you said—"

"Sporfieri? Where did you hear that name?" Now it was Hector's turn to look puzzled. "I remember the conversation, Heck, but it wasn't about any place named Sporfieri. It was about this town, the one we're staying in. Sporsazia."

Hector nodded, pretending to understand, but he was mystified. Sporsazia?

"And anyway," she went on, "I think I figured that one out. 'Spor,' from *spur*, or 'city,' and the closest thing I can find to 'sazia' is *zatlath*, Etruscan for 'companion.' So the name probably means something like 'city of the friend' or 'city of friendship.'"

Hector didn't trust himself to speak, because he didn't know whether laughter or sobs would come out of his mouth. Arath had said that everything would eventually wind up the same, just as if Hector had never traveled to the past. Well, he was wrong. At least one thing was different: the name of the town. Hector had kept Arath from being killed and so there was no human sacrifice to name the town after. Instead it had been named for a friend.

And he knew that he, Hector, was the friend, the brother from a foreign land.

"Sporsazia," he said aloud, and laughed quietly. It had a good sound.

AUTHOR'S NOTE

More than two thousand years ago, Rome was a village nestled in a crook of the Tiber River. According to Roman tradition, a man named Tarquinius Priscus became its king in 616 BCE. Tarquinius was not a Roman, but an Etruscan. The Etruscans inhabited most of the Italian peninsula and controlled a large part of its center. They called themselves Tyrrheni and said that they had originally come from Lydia, in what is now Turkey. Many ancient authors agreed. Some said, though, that the Etruscans were native to Italy, and still others thought that they were Greek immigrants. Even today nobody knows which, if any, of these theories is true.

Under the Tarquin kings (their Etruscan name was probably something like Tarchna), Rome grew into a city. The Etruscans drained the swamp that became the Roman Forum, built roads and temples, invented gladiatorial combat, made fine pottery (like the bucchero ware that Hector admired so much), and decorated their tombs with beautiful paintings of feasts and dances, of elegant horses and mysterious priests, of people hunting and fishing for impossibly rainbow-colored birds and fish. They were highly skilled craftspeople, especially in metalwork; the gold balls on their jewelry are so tiny that some museums supply a magnifying glass so that you can see the precisely formed and meticulously placed decorations on the rows of marching lions and other animals. They worshipped gods that became better known by the Roman versions of their names—Maris (Mars), Menrva (Minerva), Nethuns (Neptune), Uni (Juno)—and others like Vanth, goddess of death; Selva, god of the forest; and Lusna, the moon goddess.

Eventually, the Romans grew tired of being ruled by a series of monarchs, especially foreign ones. They expelled the Etruscan kings and established a republic with elected officials. Then there was no stopping them; the city grew and expanded until after a few centuries the Roman Empire controlled most of the known world. Much of Etruscan culture was lost, and although some well-known Romans of later times were of Etruscan origin, gradually the surviving members of that group became absorbed into the majority.

One of their most important contributions, to the Roman way of thinking anyway, were the Sibylline books. An ancient story says that a Sibyl, a woman through whom the gods spoke, approached Tarquinius Priscus and offered to sell him nine books of magic for three hundred gold coins. He refused. The Sibyl went away, burned three of the books, and then offered the remaining six to the king for the same price. Once again he refused, thinking she was crazy. So she burned three more and came back with the same offer: the remaining books (only three by now) for three hundred gold pieces. Belatedly, Tarquinius recognized that he was about to lose important magical knowledge, so he paid up. Early writers say that the rulers of Rome consulted these books in times of emergency. An ancient Greek author said, "There is no possession of the Romans, sacred or profane, which they guard so carefully as they do the Sibylline oracles." The three remaining books were eventually destroyed in a fire.

If these books or something like them really existed, what was written in them? The Etruscans were famous for being able to foretell the future by looking at the flight of birds and other natural events. One technique they used was examining the liver of a sacrificed animal. The bronze liver that Ettore mentions to Hector really exists. It is covered with writing in the Etruscan language to help the haruspex (the person who interpreted natural events) figure out what the different bumps and discolorations on the animal's liver meant. Perhaps the now-lost Sibylline books also contained instructions for foretelling the future.

The Etruscans had other ways of making predictions. One involved having a boy gaze into a mirror until he saw something that could be interpreted as a future event. Who knows if the boy actually saw something, or if he stared so long that his eyes got blurry and he imagined a scene, or if he got tired of the ritual and made up a story so that he could get away.

What if one of these boys learned how to decipher the letters in the book that was being read aloud while he was supposed to be looking in the mirror? What if that book was a copy of one of the Sibylline books that had been bought by the Etruscan king? And what if it turned out that the reason the Etruscans were so good at foretelling the future was that they actually *traveled* forward in time, saw what was going to happen, and then returned to make a prediction? By reading the sacred texts, the boy could figure out how to do this himself. A smart boy might even learn the languages and customs of the places where he time-traveled, just as Arath did in this story.

ETRUSCAN–ENGLISH GLOSSARY

The origins of the Etruscan language are as mysterious as the origins of the people themselves. The Etruscans adopted not only most of the Greek alphabet but also some Greek words (and, later, some Latin words). To form theories about the pronunciation of Etruscan, scholars have looked at which Greek letters the Etruscans used and which they omitted from their written language, and also at the pronunciation of modern Italian in the areas where the Etruscans were once powerful. They assume that similarities in pronunciation in these areas might reflect the common Etruscan ancestor of these dialects. Some of the theories on the pronunciation of different Etruscan letters are fairly secure, but others are just the best guesses that scholars can make, based on scanty evidence. The pronunciations given below are based on a chapter in *The Etruscan Language* by Giuliano Bonfante and Larissa Bonfante.

    aisar (EYE-sar). Gods.
    aisna, eisna (EYE-snah). Sacrifice.
    alpnu (AHLP-noo). Give.
    ati (AH-tee). Mother.

celu (KEH-loo). A kind of priest.

clan (clahn). Son.

cvil (kwill). Offer.

fanu (FAH-noo). Sanctuary; temple.

fler (flair). Sacrifice.

Flerchva ratum tur (FLAIRK-wa RAH-toom toor).
Carry out the sacrifice according to the law.

flere (FLAY-ray). God.

hinthial (HIN-thee-al). Spirit; ghost.

Rashna (RAHSH-nah). Etruscan.

ruva (ROO-vah). Brother.

spur (spoor). City.

thuleri (TOO-lair-ee). Beyond the borders.

turn (toorn). Given, offered, dedicated.

zatlath (TSAT-laht). Companion.

zusleva (TSOOS-lay-vah). Offering, sacrifice.

ITALIAN-ENGLISH GLOSSARY

Italian vowels are pronounced very openly. The letter *r* is trilled as in Spanish.

affresco (ah-FRES-coh). Fresco (painting made on wet plaster).

apprendista (ap-pren-DEE-stah). Apprentice.

attento (ah-TEN-toh). Be careful.

bravo (BRAH-voh). Good; well done.

bucchero (BOO-keh-roh). Black Etruscan pottery with finely incised geometric designs.

buongiorno (buohn-JOR-noh). Good morning; hello.

caffè (cah-FEH). Coffee.

cara (CAH-rah). Dear.

C'hai [Hai] ancora fame? (cheye [rhymes with *eye*] ahn-COH-rah FAH-meh). Are you still hungry?

che bello (keh BEH-loh). How beautiful.

che caldo (keh CAHL-doh). How hot it is.

ciao (chow). Hi; bye.

d'accordo (dah-COHR-doh). Agreed.

dormiva (dor-MEE-vah). He was sleeping.

è qui (eh KWEE). He's here.

ecco (EH-coh). That's it; there it is.

eh già (eh jah). Oh, right.

fiorentini (fior-en-TEE-nee). Florentines; people from Florence.

grazie (GRAH-tsieh). Thanks; thank you.

malocchio (mahl-OKE-yo). Evil eye.

molto bravo (MOLE-toh BRAH-voh). Excellent.

Permesso? (per-MEH-soh). May I come in?

rosetta (roh-ZET-tah). A crusty roll made in and near Rome.

scintillando (sheen-tee-LAHN-doh). Shining; glittering.

sì (see). Yes.

Su, andiamo! (soo, ahn-DIAH-moh). Come on, let's go!

ti adoro (tee ah-DOH-roh). I adore you.

Tu proverai si come sa di sale lo pane altrui (too proh-veh-REYE [rhymes with *eye*] see coh-meh sa dee SAH-leh loh PAH-neh al-TROO-ee). You will find out how salty other people's bread tastes.

Vieni qui! Ho trovato qualcosa! (VIEH-nee kwee! oh troh-VAH-toh kwal-COH-sah). Come here! I found something!